THE INNOCENT PARTY

THE INNOCENT PARTY

———

STORIES BY AIMEE PARKISON

AMERICAN READER SERIES, NO. 17

BOA EDITIONS, LTD. • ROCHESTER, NY • 2012

For information about permission to reuse any material from this book please contact The Permissions Company at www.permissionscompany.com or e-mail permdude@eclipse.net.

Publications by BOA Editions, Ltd.—a not-for-profit corporation under section 501 (c) (3) of the United States Internal Revenue Code—are made possible with funds from a variety of sources, including public funds from the New York State Council on the Arts, a state agency; the Literature Program of the National Endowment for the Arts; the County of Monroe, NY; the Lannan Foundation for support of the Lannan Translations Selection Series; the Mary S. Mulligan Charitable Trust; the Rochester Area Community Foundation; the Arts & Cultural Council for Greater Rochester; the Steeple-Jack Fund; the Ames-Amzalak Memorial Trust in memory of Henry Ames, Semon Amzalak and Dan Amzalak; and contributions from many individuals nationwide. See Colophon on page 184 for special individual acknowledgments.

ART WORKS.
arts.gov

State of the Arts

NYSCA

Cover Design: Sandy Knight
Interior Design and Composition: Richard Foerster
BOA Logo: Mirko

Library of Congress Cataloging-in-Publication Data

Parkison, Aimee, 1976–
The innocent party: stories / by Aimee Parkison — 1st ed.

   p. cm.
ISBN 978-1-934414-86-6 (pbk. : alk. paper)
I. Title.
PS3616.A7545I56 2012
813'.6—dc22

2011038425

BOA Editions, Ltd.
250 North Goodman Street, Suite 306
Rochester, NY 14607
www.boaeditions.org
A. Poulin, Jr., Founder (1938–1996)

for Abelardo Reyes Gurrola

CONTENTS

Paints and Papers — 9

Dummy — 19

The Glass Girl — 33

Locked Doors — 35

Murder on the Pasture — 55

Call Me Linda — 59

Warnings — 77

Allison's Idea — 95

Shrike — 115

Chains — 129

Etcher — 139

Vision of Mirrors — 159

Theater of Cruelty — 163

Acknowledgments — 177

About the Author — 179

Colophon — 184

Paints and Papers

Even before the boy attacked him, the artist preferred sleeping on the hills overlooking the shore, where the sea made sounds like whispers before the rain. In his old age, he painted as if every hour was his last, and he stored the paintings on the docks. Even though he remained alone, he felt the presence of heavenly beings all around him. The boy who tried to kill him seemed like a messenger. Even before the boy cracked the artist's skull open, the artist believed in divine inspiration. He was inspired, yet he could not see the angels until the drunken boy hit him over the head with a lead pipe.

The lead pipe did what some might call *damage*. For six days, the artist remained unconscious. On the seventh day, when he awakened in a hospital, he could not speak. Although he never fully recovered his ability to talk, he began to see what he thought were angels in every room. The angels were long angular forms of blue light leading away from the hospital. The light blurred as it moved. Occasionally, when the light stilled into focus, the artist could see faces smiling through the brightness.

He followed the angels, and the angels led him back to the shore. He began to paint drunken children whom the angels gestured to with orbs of pale light. Surrounding the children's bodies, the angels overshadowed all. The artist knew the boy was among the children, but could no longer recall his face.

Even now, the artist is with the drunken children and the angels, hiding on the hills near the shore. Angels beckon to him. His eyes ache in light that only he can see. The children don't know he is there—watching, staring, studying, sketching, painting all night and all day.

———

Using his binoculars, the artist studies the sea and sky—strokes of blue overlaid with violet paint, black and red gently washing together. His vision blurs and the sea becomes fiery. Arranging his easel, he searches for a new vantage point. Drunken children by the sea are dramatic features arresting his gaze along waves. Children rise, tiny crawling bodies diving into deep rich blue reflecting sky. The artist's binoculars have powerful lenses that never fail to reveal the children's smooth symmetrical features.

Despite all the years of practice, the best effects the artist achieves are spontaneous. As his eyes follow the children, he tilts the wet painting from side to side. His arms move like waves.

———

The hills are his studio. In the morning, as the artist watches, girls and boys pass bottles, kissing between sips. For some reason, the children suddenly seem to love each other and can't stop laughing. They slurp and burp. The colors of the shore grow more pleasing—golden sands, silvery horizon, blue waters, green trees, orange sun, white blossoms, pink clouds, bright blue sky as in a painting of a landscape where there is nothing but distant beauty.

Blossoms break apart. Pale petals drift and flutter down to waves. The girls begin to dance. Petals swirl and sway. Hips shimmy like water. Boys throw sand, glittering, falling on the girls' hair.

Unknown to the children, the artist crouches with his paints and papers on the hills. To the artist, the children are handsome luminous figures that bring a thrilling quality to his imagery. The children become symbols to the lonely man. As symbols, they convey important messages. Bringing clarity and vision, the children remain strangers to him, even though he paints and sketches and studies them for years.

With intricate masking, he captures and preserves the pure white light sparkling on water. Paint splatter becomes blossoms and leaves, crabs and shells and birds shaped by fleeting movements, impulsive sensations and reactions in his sensitive weathered hands. By creative intuition, he captures the ebb and flow of darkness along with a continual vibration of light. Touching every image, soft light falls like young hands caressing his filthy body. He falls asleep beneath the easel.

When he wakes at dawn to study his paintings, the children's flesh seems rendered in an impressionist style—pastel brush stokes that cause flesh to take on the white of blossom, the gold of sand, and the gleam of ocean. Warm sun tones bring out the blue-green and brown of intoxicated eyes. In images of those days on the shore, the drunken children seem to have no cares and no regrets. Unlike the painter, who knows exactly what he is, the children don't know they are winos.

How could children understand? Only the painter knows drinking red wine changes the shore in imperceptible ways.

At first, it paralyzes the taste buds in ecstasy as overpowering as it is relaxing. A tainted aftertaste conceals a touch of cork rot. All is masked under delicate tones of chocolate, vanilla, and raspberry with hints of dried herbs and spice.

He senses when inebriated children begin to feel the tingling. On their tongues and in their loins, the mysterious hunger brought on by wine is only an erotic joy increased by thirst. Later, sensual memories of drunken days will become a sexual elegy only the painter and the young winos know.

As they explore each other's bodies, the painter feels them moving against each other—tormented, stroking each other's flesh, never realizing they are only as lovely as they are lost. Becoming lost is what makes them exquisite, even to each other.

Searching for isolated coves, pairs of children stroll. Upon returning, they leap and scream, rushing into the sea to kiss beneath moonlit waves. As their bodies entangle, they seem unaware that angels watch as their lives slip away.

It will take them years to die by what gives them joy. In the meantime, the artist sees the young winos dancing and is revitalized, enlightened by their splendor. They remind him what it is like to be free.

He would give anything to become a child drinking stolen wine on the shore.

————

The painter believes that the wine has been placed on the shore by angels. No matter how intoxicated, the young winos will never believe what the painter has become convinced of—that the angels test the children, yet in drinking the wine, the children have failed. The angels' test will go on for years of joyous excess. The children destroy themselves with angel wine.

Slowly, then quickly, the children drink more. With every gulp, the angel wine tastes better. The wine churns and burns their little bellies, swirling inside. Their chests feel light, and they give the painter a dizzying sensation of falling from great heights, even though they are rolling on the shore. They braid each other's hair and kiss each other's backs, feet, legs, necks, shoulders, breasts, and faces. Tiny kisses land like dragonflies on water.

Angels mimic the children's wobbly stances. Angels pretend to be drunken children while laughing and singing with unheard voices.

The more wine the children drink, the better kissers the angels become. They become master kissers, locking lips in ecstasy. To the painter, the kisses are more intoxicating than the wine. The children have no idea what the kisses are doing to them, as the kisses flow from one mouth to another. They will never kiss this way again after the stolen wine is gone. No kisses and no other wine will ever live up to the memory of this day. Their lives will be ruined by joy. The initial bliss will go unmatched while angels watch, hidden in the sea. No matter how much more wine the children consume, they age. The first bliss never returns, even to those who live decades beyond the first drink.

Angels watch the painter with knowing eyes, tears glistening like stars.

Because of the expressions on the angels' intelligent faces, the painter knows that no other shore will ever seem like this shore. Once the children leave it, they will never be able to find it again.

Boys and girls pass green bottles. They spill and lick wine off each other's bodies, and the painter writhes alone in extraordinary ecstasy while painting the lovers. Studying gesture, the painter learns to capture suggestions of even the smallest sighs, the first hints of seduction, the gentlest of embraces. He becomes obsessed with painting the swimmers' legs entangling underwater—what he can only imagine and cannot see.

A midnight renewal continues until dawn. When boys carry girls across sand, they shatter glass. Laughing and crying, they hold each other. Dancing, they sway, attempting to stand. Shattering glass glimmers, emeralds on sand. Children dance barefoot among shards, cutting their feet. They fall on each other. They pick velvety white blossoms from trees. Their hands are dusty with butterfly scales.

Angels weep for the painter.

The children will always be failures. After tasting the angel wine, they become weak, loving wine more than they love work, money, food, or each other. They love the wine more than they love life itself. Intoxication becomes their birthright. Afterwards, they will always secretly suspect that all wine, like all kisses, should be glorious and free and found on any shore.

———

Although the first days linger endlessly, the last days keep getting shorter. Eventually, all of life seems short, and all the short days blur together. Later, the children wish to return to that moment of the first sip but can never find a way. The painter yawns as the wine warms him inside so that there are flames in his body. It feels good—so good, too good—so that he overflows with laughter. His breath smells like smoke as the children kiss each other, slowly, burning him with sizzling tongues.

The children fall on the sand. As the sky darkens, they sleep in each other's arms.

———

One of the children gets the idea to take off his clothes. Naked, he stands before the others. He tosses his clothes into a barrel of fire and watches the worn fabric burn. The other children think he's a genius—a naked genius. They all want to become like him, so they all follow his example. Burning all their clothes and laughing, they sip and slobber and kiss.

As ashes float into the sea, the girls cover each other's nakedness in shells like jewels.

White blossoms flutter through wind across tides. Pale petals stick to wine-soaked bodies, shimmering pebbles in sand, and the painter paints blossoms for many evenings.

Soon, more angel wine is discovered. Angels tuck bottles and bottles of wine into the grasses, nestling bottles into the nests of birds, burying them shallowly beneath sand with crabs.

The children find more hidden bottles chilling beneath waves. The painter longs to warn those who swim too far. Instead, he watches them drown. Angels' arms carry broken bodies, currents deep beneath water.

———

Children skip and fall. Waves become shawls covering girls' tiny breasts.

The stolen wine lasts for years, until the children have more children and their lazy infants swim beneath frothy waves to the painter's delight.

———

For a long time, the wine seems to keep the children alive so that they forget their longing. Because so many of them have become desensitized and can't feel anything anymore, they desire a touch beyond touch. Everything is sexual; nothing is sensual. They forget their own bodies and can no longer taste or smell, their senses dulled or gone. When they look at each other, it's as if they don't see. Everything becomes dim and hazy. They forget each other's names. They swim deeper and deeper, farther from shore. As they fade, they begin to sense the painter's presence and dream of brushstrokes.

———

Drinking from each other's mouths, the children sip from curled tongues like wet leaves. Blue-green waves conceal their nakedness, even from each other.

———

Wine changes children over time. Even though they don't realize it, as they hold each other, they become adults. They cling and moan and are no longer children. They shiver and cling to each other, as if for warmth. Yet they are cold, so cold. Something is leaving. Angels grow impatient, no longer entertained by watching winos dance. The shore changes, again, and the paintings—once full of light—become dark. One by one, winos lose each other in darkening water.

DUMMY

No one knows. I can't say why she ended up loving me during the sad years. Or, perhaps, this is why—she had a scar beneath her long hair, a hollow that no one else could see, and the fact that the scar was there changed her in ways that no one but I could understand. Only she and I knew of the scar's existence. As far as I know, I was the only one allowed to touch her there—the only one who could move back her hair and put a finger inside the hole in her skull while she laughed, her mouth wide open so I could see the cavities in her back teeth. She was beautiful and she loved me like no one else ever loved me—no big deal. Her skin and her hair smelled of the white roses that had covered her in the coffin, and I wanted to eat those white roses for dinner with a big glass of cheap red wine by candlelight.

———

There was a gated elevator in that old building where she died, a door to the outside that would not close and a window that would not open, and a dusty record turning on a player that could be heard throughout the halls on the sixth floor. The song was a dead woman singing.

"That's Karen Carpenter, Dummy," Belle said.

I remember that woman. Like a bird, she died of hunger.

People didn't speak to each other in that building. They lived too close together, and the walls were so thin I could hear toilets flushing and voices murmuring. I could have spoken to my neighbors by calling their names close to the walls, and I think that was why no one wanted to know the other people who lived there.

Later, I wondered if the other tenants thought I was responsible for the terrible thing that happened. I don't know if I was or if I could have prevented what happened in the building before the city ordered us to leave our rooms. We began to scream at each other through the walls, demanding that everyone lock the windows, demanding louder music to force out the silence.

On the sixth floor, there was a man who lived with another man and a woman who lived with another woman. No big deal—the various forms and stages of fucking played out behind closed doors like movies in an all-night theater. But I was that woman. There was also a woman who lived her life as a man and a man who lived his life as a woman. Later, I found out the woman was really a man and the man was just as much of a woman as I was. But I didn't really know them that well, and I didn't think they knew each other. They were just people who lived near me at a time when I didn't want to live near them.

Then there was Belle, the beautiful woman with a tattoo of a blue iris on her left breast. She killed herself by taking a swan dive off the building's flat roof. Her name was Jane—or rather, her name had once been Jane, before the fall—the jump, that is. She was my lover—no big deal. The night she died, I dreamed I was sitting on the balcony drinking cold coffee when a large white bird flew into my lap, its claws piercing my legs.

When I identified her body, I couldn't recognize her face because the back of her head was gone and had been replaced by a fractured brain. The blood and bone that had broken through her forehead revealed her brain in an odd pattern around her eyes resembling an owl's face peering out from under her hair. Late at night, I keep trying to visualize this, but the memory doesn't make sense anymore because she is still here in the room beside me, sleeping. She doesn't remember the night that she killed herself—or at least this is what she claims. I have my own suspicions, but the neighbors are of no help because they refuse to speak of that night and did not attend her funeral. Who could blame them? It's not like it was high-class entertainment or anything that they were missing out on.

Maybe that's not what she really looked like after she died or what most people would have seen if they looked at her head. The news report said she died instantly. But by the time I made it down the stairs, people were saying she was still alive, that she was twitching and sort of moving around like a baby on the concrete.

"Never trust the news," I say to Belle whenever she turns on the television.

"Journalists are liars," she says, "and I have the hole in my head to prove it."

There was a sheet over her body, but the sheet was not ours. I had no idea where it came from—a simple, white sheet. Outside the building, there were policemen holding other white sheets in the air around her, making a tent to conceal her from people passing by. Maybe it just looked like a brain coming out of her head, but for some reason, I didn't see it that way, probably because I knew her when she was still dancing with me, singing to her jazz records, and her brain seemed too precious to be broken apart and scattered like leftover pie thrown to pigeons. Later that night, when she came back to the apartment, her head seemed just fine, until she let me lift the long hair away from her scalp so I could see the way she was concealing the smashed skull beneath her thick curls. She had stuffed the damp hollow in her head with fresh cotton and fastened the hair over the wound in a woven crown that resembled the bun my teacher, Miss Sarah, used to wear on her head when I was in the second grade—when I had no idea that dead women were such touchy lovers.

When the day came, I thought she wouldn't go through with it. I was teasing her about it, but I got scared. During the evening, I began to get mad at her and started throwing pillows at her face. I decided I would ignore her threats and go to sleep just as if it were a normal night.

I didn't think she would jump without me. We were supposed to hold hands.

In my dream that night, I was terrified of the white bird and thought it wanted to kill me. I woke to sirens that startled the bird. Once the bird took flight in my dream, I never saw Jane alive again. Belle, however, came back. No one called her Jane anymore, and she didn't seem to mind.

I didn't want to see her in the wooden box. It was pure mahogany. Her mother and father bought it for her. When I told them I didn't want to go to the funeral, they said I should at least come to the viewing.

Her casket was displayed in a bed of blue and yellow roses. She was wearing a lavender dress and a violet veil that covered her hair and most of her face, except her mouth and chin. Her lips were closed and painted crimson. Inside the coffin, her skin was awash in white roses, the bright petals framing her slender body.

Hers were beautiful lips, and I wondered if I was seeing them for the last time, so I moved closer to the casket, pushing aside some people I didn't know. I leaned over Jane, and I touched my lips to her lips and whispered, "Can you hear me?" Then someone started yelling, "Get away from there. What are you doing? Don't touch the body."

I jumped into a taxi and traveled all over the city, trying to see some of the places she liked to go—the bars under the bridges, the streets above the river.

———

I had a lot of time on my hands. Belle and I were alone in our small apartment. I began to discover things I had never seen before. I found a photo of Jane in a white wedding dress standing next to a small man with clear blue eyes, but Belle refused to tell me who the man was. I had never seen the man before, and I had no idea Jane was ever married.

"Leave me alone, Dummy," Belle said when I asked about Jane.

She broke the glass that covered the wedding photograph by throwing the frame at the window.

I found a doll with curly red hair hidden under a pile of sweaters on Jane's side of the closet. I found a brush full of Jane's hair and held it under my nose for a long time. Then I rolled the hair into a tiny ball between the palms of my hands.

"What are you doing with that hair, Dummy?" Belle asked.

I put the hairball in my mouth and swallowed it like I would a large vitamin pill.

After I swallowed the hair, I began to run my hands all over the walls, just to know what they felt like. The paint was as rough as scar tissue in areas that had been patched over with plaster and gauze. I found a tiny hole in the bathroom wall. I prodded the hole with my fingers until it was the size of a golf ball.

When I looked through that hole, I could see into the bathroom of the apartment next to mine. A family lived there, a mother and a father and a little girl. I watched them take baths, and I didn't feel as lonely anymore. I watched them dress and comb their hair. They kissed each other and sang to each other in there sometimes. The girl must have been afraid of water. She didn't like to take baths by herself. Her parents were young, in their early thirties. The girl was about five years old. Her name was Carrie.

"Why are you watching those people?" Belle asked, making a horrified face at her reflection in the bathroom mirror. "Don't you know?" she asked.

"Know what?"

"They know you're watching them, Dummy."

Three weeks later, I watched Carrie's father crawl into the bathtub, fully clothed in a blue suit, white tie, and black shoes. He removed his glasses, sighed, then stuck a gun in his mouth but didn't pull the trigger.

"I don't want him coming in here," Belle said. "I don't want him walking through the bloody walls."

I didn't know what to do, so I called the police and ran next door, pounding on the wooden panels. No one answered. People were gathering in the hall, looking at me accusingly. When I went back to my apartment, I looked at myself in the mirror and noticed the gun barrel sticking through the hole in the bathroom wall. The gun kept moving to follow my motions. It pointed at me whichever way I went until I ran out of the bathroom.

The next time I went back to the bathroom, the gun was gone and the hole had been mended with plaster. The plaster was thick and still wet.

I saw Carrie's father in the halls three days later. He was whistling a blissful tune. He waved to me. I waved back. I asked him his name. He had a soft voice and wouldn't look me in the eye when he said, "Edgar."

———

There was a green light in the halls coming from the windows in the evenings. There were two rows of white rectangles where the ceiling lights reflected on the black floors at night. There were silver wires on the gates that would not close. There was a sign over the central stairs that read, "Don't Fall." There were people who had fallen before and would fall again. In my dreams, they were falling and were going to fall.

There were ideas that came to me in the evenings. I thought they were good ideas when they were bad ones. One had to do with a case of Korbel brandy Jane had left behind, a mellow oak, "uncommonly smooth," as the bottle labels read. I decided to drink an entire bottle every time I began to think of Jane in a sad way.

The bottles began to disappear so quickly that I wondered if Belle might have been sneaking into my room at night to drink the brandy while I slept. I became obsessed with the idea that an intruder was entering my apartment unseen. I couldn't sleep at night, wondering.

—————

Even though I no longer officially lived with Jane, since her name had been taken off the mailbox, I felt her presence constantly. When I was drinking, I refused to believe that I was ever truly alone. Sometimes I thought she might be watching me.

In darkness, I woke near the birds on the ledge, nests of straw and string. I was crouching outside my window, nude from the waist down. Looking out at the traffic below me, I clung to the ledge and tried to cover myself. I had no idea where I was at first. When I felt the night air on my vagina, I felt so exposed. I never knew how I had gotten there, what had caused me to wander out onto the ledge in my sleep.

Hoping no one had seen me, I climbed back inside. The next night, I woke in the same position, crouching on the dark ledge outside my window. Only this night, I was fully clothed in a T-shirt and blue jeans and was shocked to see other people shivering in the cold wind while huddling on the ledges outside their windows. The birds were tittering at us, fluttering over our heads. We looked at each other in silence, not knowing what to say.

Edgar was reaching out to Carrie. She was crawling toward me.

"Don't let her fall," he called out. "Can you reach her?"

"Catch her! Catch the girl!" the other tenants, who were leaning out their windows, were shouting at me.

I grabbed onto Carrie's arm and pulled her close to me. People slowly moved back to their open windows and began to pull each other into their apartments. Still holding Carrie, I helped her to my window and into my apartment. Just before I opened my apartment door to let Carrie out, Carrie looked back at Belle, who was eating pretzels and sipping diet soda on the sofa.

"Hi, Belle," Carrie said. "How are you doing?"

"Just fine, Sweetheart," Belle whispered, turning down the volume on the television.

Neither Carrie nor I could remember or explain why we had awakened on our ledges.

"You were following me, Dummy," Belle said when I asked her why.

———

A month after Jane's funeral, because I had to convince myself that Belle was really there, I had our apartment walls drilled for hidden cameras to be tacked behind light fixtures in the high corners. I rented small cameras and hired a technician to install them behind the lights.

The cameras covered every angle of the living room that was also my bedroom. I even had a camera installed in the bathroom behind the lily-shaped lamps over the sink. The cameras made me feel safe again. My constant monitoring of the videos kept Jane off my mind. I hoped the videotapes would make the brandy unnecessary.

Every morning before work, I watched the videos from the day before. I slid each tape into my old VCR and pushed the fast-forward button, watching myself eating, sleeping, bathing, and drinking alone in my room. There were videos of myself watching the videos with a bemused expression on my face.

I began to watch my image in the videos in disbelief, just as I had watched Edgar in the tub. I was waiting to see if I would live or die, if there were signs that I might take my own life. The drinking was the strongest sign. In the videos, I saw how I changed when I got drunk, how my eyes seemed ugly, unfocused, and barely open. I saw myself stumble and fall and walk sideways, crashing into furniture and walls. I saw myself from all angles and thought that when I wasn't drunk I looked like a different woman, a woman I had never seen before, a few years younger than I thought I was and also more attractive than I normally saw myself in mirrors. I didn't want that woman to die.

There were odd moments when alone in my room I found myself performing for my cameras. I rearranged my apartment's furniture and bought new, more stylish clothes and changed my hair to a lighter color. I began laughing for no reason except that I wanted to see myself happy. I wanted to watch myself living a new and better life.

I rewound the tapes. I paused them in parts I liked and watched them again and again. I began to assemble a growing collection of videos that almost took up an entire shelf.

Sometimes I felt sorry for the woman in the videos and wondered why she cried so often, why she got drunk every night. I began to remember who I was. There was no intruder, no Belle or Jane. There was only me, and when I went to work, there was only the empty room, the sunlight growing brighter before slowly fading away. Every day, I looked forward to watching the day before, all along knowing that Belle would never be there. The cameras kept her away at first. Jane always hated to have her picture taken—or at least that's what I thought. Belle, unlike Jane, eventually learned to love the cameras and began asking me to play the tapes again and again so she could watch herself dancing to the radio near the window.

————

In the mornings, she watched the gray birds with red beaks that lived on the outside ledges. Because one of my video cameras once faced the window, I can still watch the tapes of the birds fluttering in circles over her head the way they often circled their nests.

My cameras captured nothing unusual those nights except for my sleepwalking during which my mouth moved rapidly as if I was trying to speak to someone who wasn't there.

I wanted to videotape my dreams, but I didn't know how. There was no way, and the thrill of the cameras was gone. I wanted to capture something the cameras couldn't see. I spent four days alone in my apartment, eating nothing, drinking only tap water, and thinking of the city below me.

"What are you doing, Dummy?" Belle asked.

The videos of those days look just alike from one day to the next. They never captured what was really happening, but only her smiling at me in the evenings the same way she had smiled before she died, laughing too loud and showing all her teeth. There were videos of her washing her long hair and twisting a tight braid into the hollow of her head while singing, putting on mauve lipstick, kohl eyeliner, and a new dress just like the one she had worn the last night I ever saw her alive.

When it was time to make my final payment on the video equipment, the technician came to check the camera angles. He asked me what I was afraid of, and I told him I just couldn't afford the equipment, that I wanted the company to take it all back. I decided to keep the tapes. That's all.

"Who were you trying to catch in the act?" he whispered, looking at Belle, who was dusting the windows.

"What?"

"What did you think you were going to see?"

"I don't know."

"Then what were you looking for?"

"I'll guess I'll know when I see it," I said, patting my box of videotapes.

Belle and he were laughing. I laughed, too.

People were moving out day by day. I was the last one living in the building with Belle. It was so quiet every step I took echoed as I walked to my room.

I was glad the others were gone. I had no idea what to say to them. It was hard to say what I was afraid of. There were days I'd seen before that I would never see again—until I replayed the videos. The only days I had ever really lost were the ones I'd never captured.

In the evening, I wiped the dust off of Jane's photos and put on one of her old sweaters, noticing it still smelled of her daffodil perfume. I oiled the gates to the elevators so they would open without a sound. I plastered over the holes in my apartment walls, believing that I would be forcibly evicted in a month and the building would be torn down in a year and another building that looked exactly like the old one would be erected in its place.

I studied my face in the mirror and tried to put on lipstick to make it seem right. I turned on the VCR and decided to watch the tapes in the sequence they were shot. I lit a fire in the fireplace and sat near its light. In the video, I closed my eyes. My mouth was saying her name. There was no sound, but she came to me anyway.

I was drinking heavily again, whenever I felt the need for exposure. I couldn't get enough of me. I was in love again—mesmerized. That's when I realized my face was changing to a face that was not my own. My face was the one I had been missing. For a moment, I had no idea what Jane used to look like before she died. No matter how hard I tried, I couldn't remember, but I was convinced I had grown to look so much like her in my sorrow we could have been mistaken for the same woman.

"Is that really you, Jane?" I kept asking Belle.

"Dummy, Dummy," she kept saying as we watched the tapes in the darkness, the blue light washing over her face, sapphire tears trailing from her eyes.

"I'm sorry," I said. "I'm so sorry I'm so stupid."

"No, I'm the one who's sorry," Belle said while gently

combing the tangles out of my hair. "I'm sorry I had to kill myself. Well, actually, I'm not. That was a lie. But I'm sorry you have to feel the way you feel. I didn't mean for it to happen this way. But what can I do?"

"You don't have to do anything," I whispered.

"I could try to explain," she said, dropping the comb onto the stained rug, "but there are some things you'll never understand—what it's like to turn into a white bird or to change your name without warning. And how good it feels to wake up in the white sheets, knowing you've already died and you'll never have to go through that again."

"It's all right," I said, putting my hand gently on her head where I could just feel the hollow. "I don't blame you. Besides, I think it's brought us closer."

"I think you're right," she whispered, pulling my hand away from her hair and stroking my fingers.

She and I danced through the blue light all night, kissing in time to the music. When we finished dancing, we held each other without speaking, my mouth pressed tightly to hers so that we breathed the same air.

THE GLASS GIRL

On certain evenings in dark motels, she could transform her lip into the edge of the bottle, imagining her face was made of amber glass and the men paused above her only to take a drink of breath. Over the years, men drank and drank until there were only two sips left inside. They began sucking the air out of the glass that grew warm in the wrong places because of heat radiating off their hands. The men's breath along with white feathers fell over autumn winds drifting through open windows. As the chill receded, hands and dry leaves glided over shadows mingling and flitting above. Girls woke to conformed arrangements of bottlenecks, brittle stems of wineglasses shattered on the balcony stairs. Witness to her own departure in hazy mirrors, she would seek herself in other women, their singsong voices echoing through chimneys of the houses she had left behind, fingers tracing the rails of the locked stairwell. Recalling the perfume drifting through dark halls, the way scent caught in curtains along with silence, she found more intricacy and misconceptions in common things—bottles, hands, and leaves—than in labyrinths designed for deliberate confusion, as in a crowded subway, passages leading onto passages. Leaves became refuse in the winter, raked into piles for burning. In the heat of flames, one could drink from a cold bottle and still be thirsty. Looking at the leaves, one could spit whiskey into the fire and watch it flare, turning old magazines and newspapers into black feathers lost on the wind. Like a fortune-teller, one could rub coal into the creases of a woman's hands to tell her age during the years when she was still alive. Shuffling through black-and-white photographs littered with occasional sepia tones like ash on broken glass, women feared her, saying she was a man because she loved them so.

LOCKED DOORS

I. Ruby's Door

She was my sister. I was only four, and I saw it happen.

The end of August 1972, the day before her school started, she and I were catching slow insects, holding them inside an old pickle jar. We had captured a spotted hopper, a damselfly with a missing wing, and a furry tent worm. We were hoping that the damselfly might fight the spotted hopper, but they only crawled over each other, their spindly arms stroking the glass wall. I got tired of examining the blank beads of their eyes, wondering what they saw.

My sister Gale took the jar from me and began to shake it as hard as she could. The insects clinked and rattled desperately inside. When she stopped shaking the jar, the worm was dead. I put my ear to the hole in the lid and heard a high-pitched sound like a teakettle steaming. The damselfly was screaming, or at least, I *imagined* it was screaming. But that sound, either real or imagined, was enough to send chills down my arms decades later. The spotted hopper was twitching underneath the damselfly, which lay upside down, black legs writhing on tangled wings. Droplets of honey-colored goo clung to the glass. "That's blood," Gale said. "That's how insects bleed."

Just then her eyes took on a horrified expression, as if she had realized something terribly wrong. "What is it?" I asked. She threw the jar at the fence post. It shattered. "I think I just pissed myself," she said. I fell to the ground, laughing. She ripped down her shorts and squatted down in front of my face. She stayed like that a long time, her mouth barely open, her hands between her legs. Then I saw blood on her fingers and a trail trickling down her leg. Neither of us knew what to make of it. She swore me to secrecy.

Because she thought she was dying, she ran to our bedroom and turned off all the lights. After putting on her best white lace dress, she knotted her hair into a high and heavy bun then lay down on the bed, perfectly still, her arms folded over her chest.

"I will come back for you," she whispered, "a kind ghost."

I begged her not to because I was terrified of ghosts. I asked her if I could keep her body in our closet after she died, and she said I could do whatever I wanted once she was gone. I didn't know about decay then. By morning, the back of her dress was covered in blood splotches like reddish brown flowers floating on water.

"Look," I said, pointing to the ruined dress.

"What'll I do?" she asked.

After some thought, I said, "Just tell everyone it's ketchup."

But there were no secrets in our house for long. Father's mouth opened and closed like a catfish mouth when he saw her, his cigar falling to the carpet. He told me to look away from her and said he would burn the dress right away, before anyone else could see it. But Mother did see the dress and was furious. "Why didn't you tell me?" she asked, slapping Gale across the face. That was the last day Gale would ever answer to that name. Later that night, she painted the name *Ruby* in blood on the white door of the room we shared throughout childhood. No one dared to wash the blood away or to speak of the door.

II. Breakdown Door

I heard her talking to someone behind the locked door, even though I knew she was alone. It's not like she was trying to become another person. She was another person.

Depending on whom I spoke to, she was known by three names: Ruby Canyon, Marilynn Glass, and her legal name, Gale Merman. I was just Andy Merman. Or, rather, I still am. I remember being terrified as a child—terrified of my sister and terrified for my sister. I knew who Ruby was and I knew who Gale was, but I had no idea who Marilynn Glass was. Marilynn scared me more than I have ever been scared by anyone in my entire life. She scares me still. Sometimes in darkness, I see her the way she was the first time she slipped away, a sweet girl with soap-gray eyes, the blue satin ribbon in her amber hair, the frail shadow unraveling over her right eye. She used to be very careful about appearances, smoothing her neck and arms with honeysuckle lotion, flossing her teeth with green wax string, brushing her hair a hundred strokes before evening.

Her hair was so glossy and full that grown men couldn't stop their hands from reaching out to stroke her. When I was just a boy, I witnessed the most distinguished men of our town pausing with their hands hovering in midair, fingers perched above my sister's amazed eyes. Her curls were so lush and unruly that men kept gazing at her head until she felt guilty, as if she had done something wrong to demand such attention. Her luxurious mane inspired boys to follow her into many evenings. I had to look out for her, to protect my sister from their cold eyes. When we were children, the back of her head felt as soft as a sealskin coat.

Her hair was still soft and legendary when I was thirty-two years old and Ruby Canyon was thirty-nine, the night I walked the dark road to find her collapsed beside her car. Never a drinker myself, I often set out on long night walks, wondering where I might find her. I traipsed past Jimmy's One Stop, past a deer skull, a shrunken cat wailing, an open-bellied armadillo with its head smashed and tracked by tires, a broken turtle writhing on its back, covered with tiny white worms. I was scared when I saw my sister from far away, her face toward the ground, her hand reaching out to me. But I had seen her that way many times before. I decided to save her again that night by walking to her, lifting her body off the dusty road, and taking her back to the dark house.

"Be nice to me," Ruby Canyon said as I leaned over her. She had her hands in her hair, her fingers working at tangles. The night was warm, and her face was damp with sweat. She crouched down on the asphalt and leaned her head against the front tire of her car. I couldn't see her face anymore, only her long disheveled hair reaching the road-side. "I wanted to make you happy," she said.

"We were," I whispered, knowing she wouldn't believe me. That night was like all the others. Once she started in on herself, there was no stopping her. She could go on for hours, cursing herself, destroying what little she loved, tearing up her car and the rooms of her house. Every time it broke my heart to stand back and watch it happen.

"Andy, Andy, Andy," Ruby Canyon said to me.

"What?" I asked.

"Oh, God, Andy."

I walked to the other side of her car. We jokingly referred to it as the blue nightmare, a monstrosity of crushed metal, rust, and glass. At the time, I was very much into cars and motorcycles, even the crappy ones that looked like scrap piles and broke down in the middle of nowhere. I was an idiot then. I started to ignore her and began checking out her car.

The windows reflected the field and its black trees in warped ways. I saw my face grimacing ironically, my hair lost to leaves, the shadow of my beard scraggily across my sharp jaw. The clouds above her far-away house loomed darkened gold in the greenish haze of trash fires smoldering beyond us. I knew the old man on the hill would be burning his refuse in rusted barrels until early morning light. He had been poking a long charred cane into the flames on the third Wednesday of every month ever since I was just a boy and my sister was a slender girl swinging from a board roped to high branches. He was our father.

I was embarrassed by his habits and my affection for him, ashamed that everything he touched smelled of smoke and ashes. Ruby Canyon always loved flames. Her long hair looked lavender like an evening lake in orange light descending. She used to think our father was the kindest man in the world. Then he broke down the door to her room and burnt the door in a fire while Mother cried, both of them hoping to make the voices silent.

III. Door to the Mirrors in the Woods

The first time she mentioned the mirrors in the woods we were just kids fighting over the television. I wanted to watch the masked phantom. She wanted to see the ice-skating competition. I told her I hated her and her eyes looked like twin, leaf-eating beetles. Even though it was a lie, she started shaking, and I couldn't get her to stop. It really scared me the first time I saw her that way, no control over herself whatsoever. Her tongue began to lash out like the soft, pink head of a blind worm exiting her mouth, rising out of darkness, terrified by light. I tried to pry her jaw open to make the worm go back inside.

When she finally put her tongue back in her mouth, she just looked at me. "One of these days I'll be gone," she said. "No one will know how to find me."

"Where will you go?" I asked, turning off the television.

"To the mirrors in the woods," she whispered.

That night I woke in our room to find her bed empty and the window open. She was gone.

In my powder-blue pajamas, I waded through the stench of road kill to reach her, the summer wind putrid against me. The trees were black against cobalt sky, leaves tussling, glimmering like coiled hair under half-moon light. The trunks grew so close that some were knotted inside, so hunched and whirled they would die if a man tried to twist them apart.

If deer ventured out of the woods, I would have chased the animals back into the darkness. There was safety away from the light where the ground was velvet with the dust of disintegrating leaves.

I didn't know what to think when I first saw the distant brightness. The lights were out of place, a signal or a warning in the far trees. When I crept closer, I discovered the source—moonlight reflected off shards of broken mirrors that were fastened to the branches with wire. My sister stood in the middle of the circle of light, her face captured in several angled reflections.

She was talking to herself again.

"Gale, this is Ruby," I heard her say in a cheery voice. "Ruby, this is my friend Marilynn."

She hadn't seen me yet. I started to run.

The next morning she was asleep in her bed as if nothing had happened. The mirror in our room was gone.

"What do I look like?" she kept asking.

"Fine, fine," I lied. She looked strange. Her voice and hair were different again.

Over the years, I came to realize she had a problem with perception. When she was a young girl, unable to remember what her face looked like when she turned away from mirrors, she used to ask me what I thought of her hair, her dress, and the thin silver necklace resting on her collarbone. I never could say exactly what she looked like, even with her standing right before my eyes. She changed every time she came out from behind a locked door.

I kept waking in the night alone, finding her gone. My normal dreams of red balls falling from the sky and finned hummingbirds swimming among long, violet fish under the sea were replaced by nightmares of my sister losing her hair in a fire.

Now, decades later, she lives alone in a dark house that looms shakily at the highest rise where the road ends in a dusty lane that leads to her trees, her mirrors. Inside her house, the floorboards are warped and faded by sunlight and water stains. The plaster is dented. From the look of the rooms, it seems as if no one lives inside. There's no way of knowing how often she slips away to the mirrors in the woods, how many nights she actually spends inside the house she calls her own.

IV. *The Door to the Blue Car*

Old, scarred by crashes, the car kept my sister and me together because she needed me to fix it often. An ancient Plymouth with paint peeling away from its doors, it hobbled along on bald tires, jittering and diving with every rise and fall in the road. Without warning, it would die in the middle of a highway and refuse to restart.

I loved that car almost as much as I loved her, and it gave me less trouble. There was something wonderful about knowing whenever it broke down I could fix it and make it right. But sisters are nothing like cars. I should know. Once Ruby Canyon started to go wrong, I could never help her, never set her right. I could never take her apart and put her back together, never make her look the way she used to look, never make her speak the way she used to speak to me, as if I were her brother and not just some man whom she met at the bar. No matter how I tried, I could never turn Ruby back into Gale, especially after she walked offstage and into the dressing room to don Marilynn's white-blond wig.

Marilynn bought the car her last year of high school with all the money she saved from stripping at the Horny Toad, the old topless bar on Bentley's Road. In fact, after Father broke down the door to her room, my sister began to live in her car. Yet I knew she hated the car from the day she bought it off the cluttered lot. Maybe it reminded her of getting hollered at, "losing her mind and body," as she later called performing, swaying slender hips toward dollar bills.

I don't know. I wasn't there every night.

After Ruby Canyon wrecked the car the tenth time, I was convinced she had done it on purpose. She stopped stripping altogether in her early thirties. On her last night at the Horny Toad, she left the car in reverse while she danced inside, flinging her hair. The car rolled down the hill, through a rickety fence, and into a scrubby pasture where it crashed into a tree trunk wider than a man's outstretched arms. It took a long time for me to locate enough spare parts to put the car back together, but I found them after visiting eleven junkyards. In a year, I restored the car to perfect condition, repainting it that exact shade of metallic blue. The same year I fixed her car, Ruby Canyon was beyond repairing, and I realized Gale was gone for good.

V. Secret Door

No matter how she hated the car, whenever she drove, she seemed to become incredibly gorgeous, her dark hair billowing like water, her lips as glossy as her eyes. Boys called her Ruby Canyon because she had the face, eyes, body, and hair of a stripper. Just like a doll, she hardly said a word. Then through the hidden door behind the scarlet curtain, Marilynn would come onstage with white hair and laughter, demanding more money than the one with dark hair who sometimes made fun of Gale.

Men and women and boys and girls loved my sister. Many different types gravitated towards her—dancers, children, businessmen, teenage runaways, college boys, truckers, preachers, lawyers, teachers, fathers, even men who loved men and men who loved women so much they became women. My sister would go wherever they wanted, her hair flying in the breeze as she rode along silently in their pickups through the night. At the Horny Toad, she wore a different costume and dressed and undressed according to the whims of those who bought her. She was anyone's precious baby-doll reflecting flames of candles and cigarette lighters in her mechanical jeweled eyes.

"Andy, oh God, Andy."

That night she collapsed in front of her car, she was just my sister, so I reached into the car window.

I put her car in drive and started to push it down the road. "Give me a hand," I said. The car rolled slowly along. "I had that dream again last night," she said, shaking her head so her hair swung away from her eyes. She looked at me and was silent, her breath coming deeper, heavier.

I was the only one she ever really confided in. But I hated hearing about her recurring nightmare in which Marilynn Glass stood in front of a white-lit window, curtains of burgundy, black flowers. The way Ruby Canyon told it, Marilynn threw a yellow scarf over the lamp, and the whole room was bathed in golden light. Miss Glass, as Ruby sometimes called her, wore a sheer green dress that ruffled when she walked, revealing the curves of her silhouette.

"The room in the dream was wonderful," Ruby said, "except for the crying behind the walls." Marilynn put on a jazzy record, but she could still hear it, so she left the golden room, and the crying stopped. When she came back, she was holding a small child with hazel eyes. Marilynn kept calling the child "Gale" as she kissed the child's hair. Then, Marilynn stepped out onto the balcony and tossed the child over the edge without looking down.

I was scared because the dream didn't make sense unless she secretly loved a very young girl or had somehow forgotten who she was. I asked what happened after the child was thrown out the window. She said, "None of your business, Andy." If she wasn't going to tell me how it turned out, I don't know why she bothered to tell me the dream in the first place.

"What the hell's wrong with you tonight?" I asked.

"You have to know?" she asked, lighting a cigarette, the flame singeing a wisp of her hair.

"Her face was my face," I thought she whispered.

"What?" I asked, a little too forcefully. Her smoking always angered me, especially because she used it as a way to create pauses in conversation whenever I asked a question she didn't want to answer.

"I dreamed I was born dying." She lit a new cigarette with the old one.

"Fair enough," I said, remembering Gale was still a girl when she became a woman. I guess she's like most women that way. She painted the Ruby door the second evening after her blood came.

The blood was the first real barrier between us, and from that summer on, she saw me as a traitor.

VI. Dark House Doors

We had to push the car all the way to her driveway. I was exhausted. "Good God, Andy" she said, panting, "I can't push any farther." So I left her car just outside her garage and let myself into her house. The front door was always unlocked, but the bedrooms were locked inside. The house was dark because she had allowed all the lightbulbs to burn out and never replaced them with new ones. I decided to replace them quietly the next week. The floors were filthy. The two of us stumbled often, trampling bottles and stray papers under our feet.

I lit a single candle so we could make our way to the bedroom, careful to keep the flame away from her wispy hair. She unlocked the bedroom door, crept inside, and immediately fell on the bed. I went into the kitchen to see what I could throw together for dinner. After searching the cabinets, all I discovered were a few dead beetles and a single can of tomato soup.

Ruby Canyon was already asleep when I returned to the bedroom to check on her. I carried a large turquoise bowl full of deep red soup. "Can you feed yourself, honey?" I asked as I approached the bed.

"Yes," she whispered, lifting her head off the pillow. She reached for the soupspoon with her delicate hand.

"I can also bathe myself and wipe my own ass," she said.

"All right," I said. Before I left her and locked the bedroom door, I placed a porcelain bowl of water and a pink cloth on the table beside her so she could bathe her face and arms.

VII. The Door to the Green Man
It was almost midnight and I had a building to clean before dawn, but first I would have to walk back to my own house

and get my motorcycle. After I left Ruby Canyon with her soup, I ran to my bike then rode straight to work. Using my key to enter through the back door, I swept the better part of that night, cleaning the halls of the anatomy labs at the morticians' college on Cliff Street.

Because I'm a big man with lots of tattoos, I'm afraid women are afraid of me, just because I drive a motorcycle and work alone. As a night janitor, I feel like wearing a navy T-shirt with big white letters that read, *I Won't Hurt You*. And I would, but I know the T-shirt would only make women fear me more. My sister was the only woman who was never afraid of me after I got out of prison, but prison was another life. I've paid my dues for what I did to that drunken man who couldn't keep his hands out of her hair.

I was thinking of all the women's names I had tattooed on my body, and then a girl with funny red glasses walked out of an empty classroom. She screamed when she saw me watching her.

"I'm the janitor," I said. "I won't hurt you."

"Oh," she said, taking a deep breath. "You're Andy."

"Yeah."

"I'm Jessie."

I thought about the way her name would look in blue ink on my left shoulder and what image I might transform the large J into after she left me. A hook, perhaps, or even a boot of some sort.

Her short brown hair was cut straight across her forehead, her bangs falling into her eyes. She had a nice smile and a kind voice. I could tell she was a good girl, but I couldn't help but wonder what she was doing alone in the building at night.

"Burning the midnight oil?" I asked, trying to hide the tattoos on my neck. I looked down at my feet and dipped the mop into the water bucket.

"Yeah, we're about to dispose of our cadaver, and anyone who stays late to do the cleanup gets extra credit, but I'm the only one who stayed," she said with a sweet smile that showed the lovely gap in between her front teeth. "Nice tats, by the way."

She led me to the anatomy lab at the end of the hall. The large windows were what first caught my eye, the oak leaves bright under streetlights. She guided me to a far table where a cadaver was stretched out in a large black zipper bag, the flaps opened so I could see the dead man's face, arms, and part of his chest. He seemed entirely too thin, bruises and veins standing out on his arms. His head and chest were shaved, and some of the skin was cut away from his breast, revealing sticky organs and chipped, yellowed ribs. There was a terrible chemical smell that made me choke.

"Why is he so old and thin?" I asked.

Jessie ran her fingers through her short, clean hair. "Probably because he got sick and died," she said.

"Why is he green?" I asked, thinking my voice sounded slightly off, almost high-pitched.

"Oh," she said, smiling, "interesting, isn't it? People turn different colors. Everyone is unique, so their bodies react to chemicals differently."

She told me she had to crawl around the floor, using tweezers to pick up every bit of stray matter that had dropped from the body. Then she had to put all the pieces back into the body bag.

"I think I know this man," I tried to tell her. She didn't

seem to understand. "I think this man is my father. No one told me he had died."

"No," she said, ushering me out of the room. "That can't be right. Do you want to get a drink?" she asked, tucking the tweezers into her pocket. "You look like you need a drink. Is the Toad all right?"

"Yes," I said without thinking. I was still wondering if the dead man really was my father. He and I hadn't spoken for years. I was halfway wishing he really was dead, so I wouldn't have to see him ogling the dancers. In the old days when I had just begun tattooing my own body, he used to sit near the stage where Ruby danced and pretend like she wasn't his child. Years ago, I'd etched the dancers' names across my chest and later transformed the undesirable names into clouds above the tattooed angels on my belly.

That night when I went back to the old bar, I rode my motorcycle as Jessie followed in her small white car. We met just outside the Horny Toad where a green neon sign flickered, *We're getting ready. Are you?*

I had to pay a cover charge at the door, but admission for women was free, and if they came without a date, they got an endless supply of free beer just for coming inside. Jessie was the only woman who wasn't dancing, and some of the strippers tried to get her to come on stage. She wouldn't go.

At the far end of the room, a bachelor party was in full swing. I knew what that meant. All hell was about to break loose, and I just stood back, waiting for it to happen. What else could I have done? When the atmosphere first started to get bizarre, I said to Jessie, "You ready to go?" She said, "No, let's stay awhile."

A group of young men, all drunk out of their minds, surrounded the stage where a tall woman in black lingerie and high heels pranced from side to side, holding up a large white sign with the words *Real Women* printed in bold letters. Two identical twin girls followed her onto the stage and started undressing each other. They coaxed a boy with crooked teeth onto the stage and began to fiddle with his belt buckle. He was trying to act like he was enjoying it, but I saw the look in his eyes. "Hey, what's going on here?" he asked, and the strippers laughed at him.

Jessie and I left soon after. "Are you sure you're all right?" I asked as she got into her car.

"Yeah," she said.

After watching Jessie drive away, I was relieved she had left on her own, without so much as a goodnight kiss. She was a good person, very smart, and I liked her too much for kissing. I admired her so much that even though I never saw her again after that night I tattooed her name on my shoulder.

VIII. *The Door to the Body*

By the time I rode back to Ruby's house, it was already morning, just after dawn. I was surprised to find the bedroom door unlocked and wondered if someone had visited her in the night. Her hair was different, even though she seemed to be sleeping. There was just enough light coming in the window for me to see without lighting candles. I leaned close to her face.

Since she was sound asleep, I decided to caress her hair, just to smooth away some of the tangles with my fingers. It was softer and thicker than any hair I had ever felt in my life, the ideal hair for any woman to have. Whenever I stretched out a curl, it sprang back to its original coil. My finger caught on a single tangle, and I decided to make it right. I tugged at the knotted strands, gently at first because I didn't want to wake her. The tangle was stubborn and wouldn't come out. So I pulled again, harder. When she still didn't respond, I thought something was wrong. I thought she must have been numb from drinking through the night, so I decided to punish her.

I yanked the tangle one last time, as hard as I could. At first, it took me a moment to realize what had happened. I knew what I saw, but I couldn't understand what it meant. All her hair was dangling above her head from the single strand still wrapped around my finger. Her head was completely bald on the pillow, the long bulk of hair I held suspended above her, shadowing her sleeping face.

When her hand moved to touch her naked scalp, her eyes flew open. Suddenly, she was wide awake, her furious gaze directed toward me.

"I told you not to touch my hair," she said. "Now look what you've done. You just couldn't leave well enough alone, could you?"

"What do you mean?" I asked.

"Andy, Andy, Andy . . ." She began to laugh hysterically, revealing gaps in her teeth. "I fooled all the bastards who worshipped me for the way I looked."

"What did you do to your hair?"

"I shaved it off, and it feels so damned good to be bald. You wouldn't believe it!"

"You're ugly," I said, so angry I didn't realize what I was saying. "The ugliest woman I've ever seen."

She ran out of the room. It took a long time to find her, even though I knew she was somewhere inside the house. I heard a rustling from inside the fireplace and saw her crouching in the ashes. "I'm sorry," I said, holding the wig out to her. She threw something little and hard at my face. It felt like a pebble hitting me right under my eye. When I picked it up off the tile, I saw it was just a fake fingernail like the kind she glued on her pinkies.

After I helped her glue the nail back on, we held each other, without speaking. Then I took off my work shirt and let her find the women's names in the clouds above the angels, my sister's fingers gliding over the letters on my chest. Before I let go of her, I told her we would be all right, that she didn't have to hide anything from me anymore, that she could do anything she wanted to herself, and we would get through together somehow.

I told her that no matter what she did, no matter what happened to us, I would never hide her name in a cloud. All three of her names were etched deep on my arms.

IX. *The Stupid Kid's Door, or The Door to My Childhood*

Ruby, Marilynn, and Gale—they are all alive in her. My sister, who is not insane, is a bald woman with a history of wondrous hair, a woman who thinks too much about becoming other women. To me, she is just like every performer I knew in this town or any other. She always wanted to save herself, but she had no idea who she was.

When she danced on the mirrored stage, she was everywhere and nowhere at once. She was any type of woman the men wanted her to be.

"No one knows our secret thoughts, our dreams, unless we tell them," Marilynn once leaned down and whispered to me before walking offstage, gathering her tips and thrown clothes.

"I guess," I whispered, looking down at my boots and imagining that we were children.

When she reappeared on stage, she was wearing a white wedding veil. It was hard to see her dancing and to realize she often pretended to be a bride when she was a young girl.

When she was ten and I was barely three, we had a fake wedding in our backyard, saying our vows behind the tool shed, the roof-tip shadow barely touching her toes. I never wanted to let go of her strong arms as she lifted me high into the air above her. My face shadowed her face. As she kissed me and swung me through the air, she was so much bigger than me, and she was still Gale Merman.

For years, I thought the wedding was real. I walked all over town, bragging to everyone that she was my wife and I was her husband. We took baths together and slept in the same bed. I kissed her at night. I held her hand whenever we crossed the street. I saw no difference between our marriage and our parents' marriage. I was proud of Gale, so I was wounded when she pulled my ears and said, "Are you crazy, boy? Why don't you shut your trap?"

I didn't understand why people were laughing at us. "Why that's your sister," some people said. Others asked if I knew right from wrong or simply laughed, insisting we were too young to be married. Looking back, I think maybe we really were married.

Because I was a child when I was her husband, hers

were the first names written on my body. With hidden needles and stolen pens, I tattooed her names on my arms the nights she left without warning.

Even though everything has changed, I know who I am.

Inside this huge tattooed man is just a stupid kid who wanted to marry his own sister. That's what keeps me awake at night.

After fearing her and loving her for so long, I'm convinced that no dreamer can ever tell a nightmare the way it was. The words we use for dreams don't make sense because our dreams unfold in wordless ways.

MURDER ON THE PASTURE

Inside the house was heat, yellow-fire lamps, or white evening light from the window. Outside whirled the dust where grackles dove, landing under pear trees. Catfish swam in the pond as frogs died, stone reflected in water. Tiny fish, silver swirling, lost in the dark wake, later writhed in the old stream that turned to dust that drought year, that summer of children pumping water, scarves tied around their mouths. Now is long ago, Oklahoma in August, a fulcrum raging when I drank my hunger back to life. Wind takes dresses off clotheslines, hats off women's hair. Rusted roofs fly off tin sheds, slicing air, catching on gnarled branches. Touch the door to my old house and you're in this, too. Red paint peels like skin. You're here and so are the others you can't see, touching your face, hands of light and window, hair of tumbleweeds, tongues of feathers, bodies of water. Croplands stretch around dirt roads that take you places you never wanted to go, past the home tracks, anonymous child, no future, no past but what the land brings. My life twists the rain's path. My father swings from a tree, my mother hangs in a dark closet. Her body becomes a pendulum—the house, a great clock. Her neck snaps under rope, her spine unravels like twine as her heart stops the old gears. Think of the slaughter, bodies long retired to shadow, blood—a blue stain on the tangle of hair. I don't know all the dead, but I know the dust veiling the backcountry, a film of shed skin. My house was a hideout then, the first time I touched the doorknob and put my fingers through holes in the walls. In the great canyon called darkness, stray voices echo strange like rain in drought season. The first drops might be your imagination, not like everything else in this world past Daddy's old house, photos of the living, the dead, kept in the dark. I crack a whip, I crack a smile, taking cigarette ashes and eye twitches along with rats' nests, forgotten dances, leaves rustling over hair. Sometimes, I take on the voice of God in heaven at the street-side chapel—long abandoned, scarred by flame, dust of ages flooded with golden light. At the fallen gate guarded by tumbled headstones, I take your hand, begging you to come back as a child. Your voice is mist rising through wheat. This land is already sold and has been bought a hundred times by men whose skulls cave under dirt. The past is the pasture. Think of me. Alone and unprotected, I joined the wanderers who left everything but the idea of leaving, insects stealing bread in shawl, taking food no one else wanted. Under endless sky, I opened my legs to anyone. Thief in the night, there's room enough under any rock for the both of us. Dust is a wedding veil, my face bent down to your lips. Put your fingers on my tongue. My mouth is cold and empty. Reach into my throat. I was a girl with long hair, seventeen summers, my heart preserved in a jar of plums, still beating under glass. Think of the silver apples that became my eyes, light touching gray irises like old coins. My nipples withered, dried cherries hung above your door. Take my voice, words falling softly as ashes dusted my wrists, long bones thrown to dogs. Decay is the land's secret. Longevity is mine. I've traveled so far to come back to this place. Think of me at sundown. Taking nothing, I touch you with hands of air. I speak better now that I'm silent.

CALL ME LINDA

Even though I told people to call me Linda, that was another girl's name. I had to change my name several times because of what I had done, or rather what had been done to me. The first thing I did when I struck out on my own was to buy a great big house like I had always dreamed of. Eighty-Seven Lakelock Street was the largest house in Hidden Pond, three-stories high with a flat, gated roof. The rest of the neighborhood loomed below me—aqua pools with concrete steps leading into their water, sparrows landing on the wire over the tomato gardens, peaked roofs sagging under the cottonwoods, their shadows riddled with cats.

When I first noticed the large black bird in the house next door, I was standing on my roof and looking into my neighbors' windows. I had been watching a girl in a rocking chair, her back toward me. The TV flickered blue across her raven's shiny wings as the great bird darted through the pale light inside. When the girl caught the raven, lifted it high in her arms, and danced across the room, I began to feel a longing so profound that I beckoned to her when I saw her face near the window. Sometimes I thought she saw me waving. I never knew for sure.

Maybe I was a fool, but there was no harm in what I was doing. The girl I watched was named Gabby Wilson. She was the only one that summer. I often stood alone in my front yard, pretending to trim the hedges.

"Now," I heard Gabby's mother saying, "settle that thing down."

Then I heard a crash like a plate hitting the window, saw shadows wrestling.

"Stop!" I heard Gabby shouting back.

"I'm afraid! Please, God, don't let it hurt me!"

"Leave her alone!"

As the voices escalated the bird dove out of the house and wove through sunlight and shadow. Gabby ran out of the house as well, and I climbed the fire escape to my roof where I could watch her and the raven as often as I wanted, safe from her mother's gaze. Gabby was a slender girl with long hair sometimes worn down, sometimes twisted in a high bun. She looked like a ballerina from far away as the raven landed on her outstretched hands. Her arms were like slender branches, her body like a little tree to the large bird that could have torn out her lovely eyes.

One neighbor woman whom I didn't care for much because of her condescending tone was Mrs. Myers. According to her, Gabby was a "corvidophile." Mrs. Myers seemed delighted to say the word, which I had never heard before. Because of her tone, I thought *corvidophile* was a fancy term for *pedophile*. I thought of Hope, my long ago stepmother, with whom I had once had a bond that most would consider criminal, and felt afraid.

"Corvidophile?" I asked.

"Yes," answered Mrs. Myers. "She loves the raven and she loved the dead murder, a swarm of crows and some crippled, the only things she ever cared for besides that raven of hers. A boy from our neighborhood shot the last crow dead, and I suppose some were glad."

"Why?"

"Who knows?"

"Was he sorry?"

She didn't answer.

Then she whispered, "You know it's illegal for her to have that thing in her house. It's a crime. I don't know why it hasn't been reported."

Whenever I tried to look Mrs. Myers in the eye, she looked to the swing's shadow drifting over Gabby's porch. I suppose many people mistrusted Gabby because of the scavengers she had chosen to love. She seemed to be getting thinner by the day, and I assumed this was because she was mourning the birds she had lost. She wore long dresses and dyed her hair strange and mournful colors—black, blue, purple, and green—all the colors of the raven's wings. The thinner Gabby became and the stranger the colors she wore, the more beautiful she was to me. The more elusive she was, the more I wanted to know her. I came to feel that I had somehow bought my house to be close to her.

I didn't want Gabby to know the truth about me. I had left Georgia to get away from Hope, my first and only lover, who told me I had failed her. She had pinned all her hopes on Father, and he had cracked under the pressure. He found work as a school bus driver and a florist's assistant, arranging tropical flowers in a small, white room. Hope was too young to be a good stepmother anyway. As she held me close in the night, she drove my father away, farther and farther into the quiet darknesses of our sprawling house.

Ten years after he left us, Hope said she could love me the way she loved a man. We were in bed when she said it. Of course, I didn't believe her.

I was twenty-seven the night I drove away. Within a year she died—the body washed up along the pond's shore where we often swam at night. The neighbors had no idea what she was to me. What we were to each other.

At first, I had no idea where I wanted to live without her. I thought I would know the right house by the way I felt walking through the inside. The house on Lakelock Street felt like a place where the memories would never find me. Once I imagined I would entertain new friends, talking and laughing through the rooms without stumbling under the weight of Hope's disapproving gaze. But I was wrong about many things when it came to other people and me. After Hope died, I found myself distrusting men and wanting to hide from women the same way I had hidden from her.

Gabby Wilson was different. I kept expecting Gabby to slip away unseen, just like I did from Hope. I wanted to be the one she ran to, so after talking to Mrs. Myers, I made sure there was plenty of room inside my house for Gabby and her raven.

Everything I owned had become a mystery to me after moving, the house full of boxes I was afraid to open. I thought if the boxes contained my father's possessions I would find out things about him that I had never known about myself.

I decided to buy new clothes rather than unpack. I began thinking of ways to get rid of the boxes without causing suspicion among the neighbors. Just as I began moving the boxes into the corners, dull footsteps sounded outside the window. I opened the door. A boy who looked about eight years old smiled nervously then stumbled in. His jacket was torn, the sleeves badly mended. His jeans were covered in oil and black powder.

"Gabby's after me," he said, pulling me to the window.

I saw the reflection of my eyes in the glass. It made me sad to see my own face.

But just across the street, Gabby Wilson was clapping her hands, whistling, trying to get her raven's attention. She lifted my spirits somewhat, reminding me of how happy I once was, bicycling with Hope to my old house and later at night talking to Father while Hope braided her long hair. I thought of Hope's hair often after I left her—her blond turning gray and the delicate floral scent of her braid laced with sweat and rose perfume. Maybe that's why I liked the way Gabby's dull blue hair fell soft over her arms. Her hair was so different from Hope's, so marvelously false, so oddly colored. Listening to Gabby's voice, I forgot about hiding mine.

"What's her raven's name?" I asked.

"Lenore," the boy said with contempt.

"How wonderful," I said.

I longed to talk to both her and her raven, to feed the bird, and to carry it on my shoulder.

Outside the window, her green skirt flashed up over her ankles as she ran, her high heels digging into the ground. Where I had come from, women didn't dress like Gabby anymore. She looked like a child who had just become a woman. I knew how long skirts could hide a woman's body, or even distort her legs, tricking the eye with fabric rippling in the wind. I wondered how old Gabby really was, whether she was young enough to still be living with her mother, or whether she was like me.

"Don't let her see me," the boy said. He crouched behind me. "Don't let her know we're watching."

He reached into one of my boxes.

"Don't," I said.

Gabby looked in our direction. I almost stepped away from the window, ashamed of finally being discovered, but I waved to her at the last moment. She didn't wave back, but instead covered Lenore's chest in kisses.

"She always does that," the boy said, stepping away from the boxes. "She makes love to her raven because no one else will have her." I didn't believe what he was saying. He had dark, curly hair and large blue eyes that worried me.

"What's your name?" I asked.

"Isaac Blue," he said.

"You're the one who shot Gabby's crows?"

"What if I did?"

I thought about opening the door and calling Gabby over. I didn't want her thinking I was protecting him.

———

Gabby looked up at my roof. "I've seen you before," she whispered.

I asked, "Are you sure?"

She closed her eyes. Standing very still, she put a hand over her throat. She opened her mouth. Her teeth were transparent at the edges like wax shaved off of a candle.

"I've lost my raven," she said. "You haven't seen her?"

"Lenore?" I asked.

Gabby nodded, shading her eyes with her hand.

"No," I said. "I haven't seen her, but I'll help you look."

She let me go with her. I measured the distance we walked by the chalk drawings we passed by on the sidewalks. I walked over a yellow sun smiling, a green heart, a dollar sign, a blue cat leaping over a rainbow, a white star hanging over the name April, a little purple dragon with a beard. Gabby tromped over all these childish drawings, her spiked heels pounding.

She suddenly stopped, put her hands over her small chest and made a low, moaning cry. At first, I thought something was wrong with her heart. Then I saw Isaac sauntering out of a tree-lined yard, carrying Lenore in his arms, her feathers flicking and her small tongue peaking through the open beak.

He was smiling proudly, as if he expected us to be glad to see him. I felt a terrible heaviness sinking under my ribs as he approached. I had never seen Lenore in full daylight, and she was shivering as Isaac held her over his head.

"Put her down," Gabby yelled, rushing toward him.

"Okay," he said, surprised at the force of her anger.

"Now," Gabby said as he began stroking Lenore's silky neck. "Give me my raven." Gabby reached out to Isaac as if to take Lenore from his arms but slapped his face instead.

The raven leapt onto Gabby's hand. Isaac reared back, turning toward me, his mouth twisted, and his eyes bright with tears. The imprint of Gabby's fingers grew red on his cheek.

Out of her purse, Gabby withdrew a bloody sack and emptied the carcass of a dead rabbit onto the grass. The raven fed on the bloody meat, its gore glistening on the bird's black beak.

"Why?" Isaac asked me.

After cleaning the rabbit's bones with remarkable speed and agility, Lenore dove down into the weeds near Gabby's shoes.

"Look," Isaac said. "She can't even fly far. She's not free."

"She doesn't want to fly away," Gabby said, picking Lenore up and cradling her in her scrawny arms. "She loves me too much to leave me."

Isaac said, "I don't think so."

Gabby turned away and began to cry. She motioned to Lenore to land on her wrist then ran into the trees and sat in the shade, wrapping the bird in the burgundy folds of her dress.

"Why do you talk to her that way?" I asked Isaac. I couldn't help but wonder if he realized what malice his words held or if his animosity was genuine. I kept asking myself how at such a young age a boy could have developed hatred. For many years, I believed that hatred was linked to desire. I often wondered if my father had somehow loved Hope more, if he had stayed home with her at night, would she have ever started to stare at me in the dark when I was sleeping in my room?

"She's a liar," Isaac said, touching his cheek.

"What's the matter with you?" I asked.

"She hit me," he said, kicking the grass. "I found her raven, and she didn't even give me a reward."

"Go home," I said, "and think about what you did to the crows."

As he ran away, he picked up a small rock and threw it down the street. It broke apart on the asphalt.

At night, Gabby climbed the ladder to my roof, balancing Lenore on her shoulder. "Is it all right if we come up here?" she asked. "My house looks so small I think the wind could tear it down," she said. "You can see us from up here, can't you?"

Her hair looked purplish in the moonlight as it was taken up by the breeze. I couldn't see her face. Because of the way her voice rose, I thought she was smiling. I tried to pull her away from the roof's gated edge, afraid her hair would get caught in the wire. Her elbows felt like small balls of steel hidden under her sleeves.

When she turned around to me, her eyes were so green they glistened. The notches of her collarbone surfaced and dove as she breathed.

"Do you want to know what really makes me sad?" she asked, holding her eyelid open with two fingers, pinching out a colored contact. The lens rested like a water drop on her finger.

"Your eyes are brown," I said. In the floodlights, I saw her irises were full of gold lines radiating from their centers like a crack in a window shaped like a star. For the first time, I leaned close enough to her face to see the fine wrinkles haloing her eyelids like Hope's, cradling white makeup, caked in pale powder.

"And my hair isn't usually auburn like this. It's naturally blond, but it's really any color I want it to be. I think I'll do it again. Next time maybe red, maybe purple."

"I'd like to see you cut it short. Long hair is easy to hide behind."

"You don't have to worry about me," she said, standing tall, her feet arched. "I won't tell anyone what you're really doing."

I was reaching out to touch her hair when Lenore began to hiss at me. I stepped away, afraid Lenore might bite.

Gabby and I spent the whole night on my roof—the two of us wrapped in separate blankets, our feet almost touching. Lenore was with us always, watching from the near tree. After Gabby fell asleep, I thought about waking her up while it was still too dark for us to see each other's faces. I wondered if she knew she was turned away from me. I had only wanted to hold her arms and run my fingers through her hair while she was sleeping. I reached out for this young woman's body but touched what felt like long pipes, copper wire, and twigs under a scarf.

———

At sunrise, Gabby wasn't looking at her house or at me but higher up at Lenore swooping below a feather cloud drifting over us in the autumn sky. I reached out to touch Gabby's shoulder, and the raven leapt down onto a near branch of the oak tree that shaded us. Gabby called to the raven, and it fluttered back to her, landing on my hand as I caressed her arm. The raven felt powerful as it gripped me. I felt the warmth of its feet and was afraid to look into its eyes.

"Lenore was the reason the crows first came to us. They didn't understand her, why she clung to me. They were curious. I fed them bread crumbs until they were gentle, huge, and tame. So tame," she said, "they couldn't fly fast away. And Isaac shot them, when they were probably flying toward him, thinking he was bringing food."

"I haven't eaten meat since I was nine," she said, suddenly, "haven't touched butter, eggs, milk, or cheese since I was twelve. See these?" she asked, grabbing her small breasts in her hands. "Grown on nothing but vegetables."

"I'm so sorry," I whispered.

Gabby started to laugh, and Lenore echoed her laughter with a haunting cackle that drifted through the trees.

I tried to imagine the crows hobbling toward Lenore, their wings harboring naked hunger. Instead, I saw the shadows darkening under Hope's tired eyes, her cheekbones growing harsher as her skeleton began to rise under her diminishing skin. Every time I tried to talk to Gabby, I recognized the sound of Hope's voice.

In the late afternoon, I found myself alone on the edge of a clear pond. There were no feathers tangled in the reeds, no children's footprints marring the banks.

Isaac, hiding behind a tree trunk, smiled at me. His eyes seemed too bright. The pond smelled of wind before rain. I reached out to toss a rock into its water. Isaac stepped away from the tree so suddenly my heart murmured when I heard the sticks breaking under his shoes.

I was beginning to realize he was no ordinary boy. He had known something wonderful and terrible, what it felt like to kill a creature as dark and numerous and common as a crow, what it felt like to destroy something that seemingly would never be missed, the very feeling I had not known in all my years.

"What do you want from me?" Isaac asked. His eyes opened wider, scanning.

As I approached him, he opened his mouth as if to scream. I backed away.

"We're friends, aren't we?" I asked.

"I don't know," he said, his voice muffled under his hands. He was moving away, reeds trampled under his shoes.

"Why did you do it?" I asked him.

"What?"

"What you did to those crows. Was it just an accident?"

"No," he said.

———

The next night, I heard Gabby climbing my ladder, her bare feet falling soft on the metal. I saw the moonlight filtered through her splayed fingers. She was holding Lenore and her sandals clumsily in one arm and touching the top of the wall with the other. Her hand reached over the edge, and I grabbed on to it, pulling her onto the roof.

She was wearing a white dress, a stark contrast to the indigo feathers. As I leaned close to her face, I was suddenly afraid the raven would gouge out my eyes. Gabby's eyes were brown again. Her hair was the color of smoke rising from a sulfur flame, green and yellow mixed with gray.

Lenore raced from one corner of the roof to another then back to Gabby, the outline of her wings glistening in moonlight. I heard the raven landing at my feet and a far-away rumbling I took for thunder.

"Smells like rain," I said, touching Lenore on the beak. The raven then barked at me and scampered playfully behind Gabby's legs.

Gabby held my arm. She leaned back to catch the first drops in her mouth. "Umm," she said, sticking out her tongue and slipping it back through her lips. She closed her eyes. "That tastes good."

The rain began to fall harder and drenched us. Lenore shuddered, ruffling her feathers to shake off the rain. Lique-fied blue powder was running off Gabby's eyelids onto her cheeks. Her hair dye was slowly rinsing away, uncovering layers of auburn, green, blue, and gold. I could see the out-line of her small, sharp breasts puckering beneath her dress. All the colors of her hair and eyes began bleeding into the white fabric, splotching it yellow, black, and gray.

"What is it?" Gabby asked, putting her arms around her chest. "Why are you looking at me like that?"

"No reason," I said.

"My dress is ruined," she whispered. She reached for the zipper as if she were about to take the dress off. "And Lenore is probably cold."

"Wait," I said, not wanting to stay out in the rain.

Gabby turned on the lights. All my belongings were still packed in boxes. There were no carpets and no chairs, only the couch and tables. The rooms were so bare that when we talked our voices echoed off the walls along with the clatter of Lenore rushing through the hall.

Gabby began to wiggle her shoulders, slipping her arms out of the dress.

"Any room is fine for you to change in," I said, turning away from her.

Before I knew it, the dress was at her feet. So were her tangled stockings and her beige bra, the straps unwinding. She still wore her sandals. Her knees wobbled as she nudged the bra with her heel. I saw her ribs surfacing and receding with every breath she took.

Her arms and legs were long and frail like branches bleached by the sun. Below her thighs, the secret dark hairs were heavy with rain. Even though she was naked, she was clothed in all the colors still dripping from her.

"Hey, what's the matter?" she asked, shivering.

I looked away from her, first at my feet, then at the water stains on the ceiling. I was afraid of touching her body, the peaks of her hip bones jutting through her skin, the ribs that might have been like piano keys under my fingers, the tiny breasts she cradled in her delicate arms.

"Is there something wrong?" she asked. Although I wasn't looking at her, I knew she had finally seen me for the person I truly was.

———

I didn't see Gabby until a week later. All the curtains had been drawn at her house. I was about to give up on her until one night I heard the gasp of the back window opening and saw her slipping away. She was wearing a yellow dress I had never seen before. Her hair was cut short, curly magenta locks bouncing over her neck as she ran. Lenore was the dark shadow that followed the sound of sandals clattering.

The edge of Gabby's dress fluttered away from her legs, rustling. She stopped in front of a red-brick house with green trim. A tiny bicycle was parked against the front door under the clanging wind chimes. Gabby walked steadily across the lawn, through the shadows of the leaves cast by street-light, to a window where two small hands were pressed to the glass. I was right behind her.

Lenore tapped her beak on the screen just as I began to stroke Gabby's shoulder.

"Where are you going?" I asked.

"Where I used to go every night," she said.

A little boy was looking up at us, his mouth flattened against the window, his eyes the color of the night. "Isaac," I said, tapping on the glass, "open the window."

He slid the glass up and touched Lenore through the screen. "Gabby, please," he said. "I need to get some sleep."

I could see into his room where model eagles were hanging from the ceiling. A stuffed tiger was sitting in a chair next to the rifle propped up in the corner. Baseball cards were scattered on the floor around Isaac's feet. He was wearing red pajamas with a white helicopter embroidered on the chest.

"I haven't been able to sleep at night since you did it," she said.

"Hi, Isaac," I said, patting his hands through the screen. "Remember me?"

"Yes." He made kissing sounds at Lenore and leaned over so her beak could touch his lips.

"How could you do it, Isaac?" Gabby asked, pulling Lenore back.

"I already said I'm sorry," he said, looking at Lenore. "When do I get my reward?"

"You don't."

"But I found your raven."

"He's right," I said, putting my face near Gabby's hair. It smelled of fresh basil.

"I already know what I want," he said.

"What?" Gabby asked.

"For you to forgive me and leave me alone."

"No way."

"It was my birthday present," Isaac said, looking at the corner where the rifle rested. "I had never shot anything before."

"Wait," I said. "All right. We'll leave you alone if you just tell us why you did it."

"Did what?" he asked.

"Shot the crows."

"Because I liked them," he said.

He closed the window. Gabby and I watched him climb into bed and pull the blankets over his feet.

Lenore flew circles above the streets as we returned to our houses. I put my hand under the yellow sleeve and grasped Gabby's arm.

"She was an orphan," Gabby whispered. "But when you feed a creature who prefers fresh meat, you realize blood flows like water."

I was hoping there would be no more secrets like this between us. But I kept quiet on the way back to our houses, imagining what it must have been like for Isaac Blue on his birthday, walking with his new rifle. Then I imagined Hope drowning and decided to remember her that way.

The moment I forgave Hope, I was holding Gabby's hand.

As I watched Lenore soar, Gabby had no way of knowing that I was envisioning Isaac looking through his rifle's scope for the first time: a circle of weeds, a cluster of driftwood, an eyeful of scummy water, a patch of scraggly leaves. And then, when the scope lit on the crows, the rush of distance. Each creature traveling indistinguishable from the others. Nameless, homeless, myriad, free. Unprotected and unspoken for, they found a way to change us from far away, a swoop of dark wings across gray sky.

WARNINGS

Spinning the wrong way, knocking over chairs and slender floor lamps, smacking head into bar, losing balance, and disturbing the other dancers, I spoke with my body like my mother before me, her mother before her, and my younger sisters Tracy, Pia, and Valerie leaping off the fireplace. My family was fidgety yet agile, responding to music rather than words, bored with laughter, sick of jokes, and too afraid to cry. The women, at least, had practically given up on reading and conversation.

We were hip-and-thigh clashing in dark halls. Boom-bam! Just like that, we collapsed onto sofa or chair, callused soles still stomping to the beat. Sometimes we collided by accident, at night, thumping heads against battered walls. Music was never silenced (at least not by us), the radio never turned off. Even in sleep, our feet kicked up to a familiar chorus. Upon waking, our hands clapped to drums, and our hair flailed to screaming guitars. One sister was always calling to another, "Turn up the music!" even when one sister couldn't hear what the other was shouting because the radio was already loud.

If the record player was broken and the radio was stolen, we danced to the music of ceiling fans, running water, toilets flushing, teakettles steaming, and wind rushing through open windows. We sang so loud our throats tasted of fresh blood. When we lost our voices and the water ran out and the electricity got cut off and the wind didn't blow, we still had the memory of the old music in our heads, callused feet to stomp, pots to clang, and hands to clap.

Granted, there were noise complaints from the neighbors, just the standard "disturbing the peace" warnings that no cops ever bothered to enforce—for many reasons. My mother's house was in the country, away from city lines where ordinances could be used against us. The police knew us well, and when they came to see what all the fuss was about, they liked what they saw—me and my sisters dancing in our underwear even though we were too old to go without clothes. Our bras were pretty with tiny bows, polka dots, leopard prints, and lace. We liked to show off. We would have happily been interviewed starkers while the police questioned us for their paperwork.

Once the complaints came to nothing and the police started coming by regularly for dinner, the neighbors stopped their bitching. At least for my family, the only thing that ever disturbed our peace was the silence and stillness of the sheriff's sleep when I was oceans away from my sisters on his waterbed's waves, and yet my hands were still moving in time to my sisters' songs.

In the nights when there was silence because the sheriff turned off the radio, the songs were still running through my mind. I swayed my hips, twirling while we were apart. I obeyed a strange choreography while the sheriff turned away or left without warning, never becoming part of the music. Or, as my mother would say, the music never became part of Michael. He was gone too soon.

"So be it," she would whisper in the short silence between songs. "We are who we are."

There was a lot of truth to what she said, I suppose, even though it could mean something different to anyone at any time.

Little Bit, they called me at home because I had a butt smaller than two baseballs glued together. All that shaking kept me slender and nimble. Because I could dance without thinking, the hardest thing was to stay still. Maybe that's why I could never learn much at school.

Pigeon-toed with slightly twisted fingers and wicked ingrown toenails that even cats were afraid of, a natural-born left-handed child converted to a right-handed writer, a dyslexic insomniac, and a chronic daydreamer, I had my challenges like anybody else. For one thing, it took me a while to learn to read so I was always behind the other kids in my class.

My childhood in South Carolina was a hoot, except for kindergarten where connect-the-dots and coloring were a problem because my left hand kept reaching out to take the pencil or crayon from my right. Since I was a sloppy writer and an unconventional colorist, creating purple sheep instead of white, I was one of those kids who had to be taken out into the hall, away from the rest of the class, so I could be watched by a special teacher who gave me blue candy I took home to give to Valerie, Tracy, and Pia. All of our mouths turned blue in the evenings after school. Even my mother's mouth was stained.

Mrs. Defferies devoted her entire day to me on Mondays and Fridays of each week, making sure I kept my left hand tucked between my knees, always hidden in the folds of my skirt under the table. In a soft and patient voice, she explained to me why I should use the white crayon to color the white sheep a whiter white.

Maybe I wasn't ever much of a student until she discovered I would do just about anything for candy. Nothing was ever easy for me. I did things the hard way and appreciated minor accomplishments like learning to tie my shoes in the fifth grade. Somehow, I always got by.

Eventually, even Mrs. Defferies had to admit I had done all right. At least that's what she used to say before her son took out a shotgun and killed her one night at her home so she didn't come back to school anymore. That was the end of the blue candy. But all this was several years ago, and her son isn't even in jail now because he was young at the time. Being naturally curious, I kept wondering about what really happened. I wanted to know the story the newspapers hadn't told, but once Michael showed me the crime-scene photos, I was sorry I had seen her because I realized it was a family matter and none of my business.

The letters are still mixed up in my head. I still have a problem with b's and d's and P's and 9's, but I remember what Mrs. Defferies taught me, so everything turned out okay. I remember her like no one else does because sometimes when I close my eyes I try to put her face back together the way I have to keep rearranging the letters in the words she taught me. I learned to quit thinking so hard, just to do what I was told. Then I learned to remember her face the way it was when she was still alive. That way, everyone would think that I understood and that I had done all right. And, as I soon discovered, if everyone thought that, then I had.

———

Perhaps because I had such a deep reverence for cops when I began high school, I started "looking at men for the wrong reasons" and for that matter, the wrong men, or so my mother said. "Cops aren't dating material," she often warned me. "You make one wrong move at the right time, and then you've had it." If I was to have any man, she said, I needed a man who wasn't afraid to dance, our way. I needed a man who wasn't ashamed to look my mother in the eye and didn't need to turn on his sirens when he drove away. The police light turned the trunks of the oak trees red and blue as we raced by, and I had the rush of feeling like a criminal while I turned him into one.

At the time, the sheriff's dancing was the least of my worries. My sisters and I still danced so much that I often forgot Michael had no sense of rhythm. Because dancing was the farthest thing from my mind when I fell in love, I would have settled for any man who knew what it was to be a smart person who thought in backwards ways.

"Why do you dance?" I sometimes asked my mother. So embarrassed by the way she moved, I used to try to put my hands over my ears to shut out the music so I wouldn't be tempted to do the same. Sometimes I just forgot to shut it out, and the next thing I knew, I was spinning and tumbling like her, kicking up my legs, one at a time, hoping my pointed toes would somehow reach above my head.

Secretly, I began to attempt her moves. There were ways to dance without being seen and ways to be seen dancing without having to try. The key was never to look into mirrors.

———

Tangling shadows blocked the dirt lanes at night. Anyone who visited our neighborhood besides us was usually doing worse than we were—talking in parked cars.

Michael Lilligh sometimes drove his sheriff's car through darkness, then parked someplace close to my house, and called for me to join him.

Sometimes I hid where the tattered mimosas swayed and watched their hairy flowers drift inevitably toward the ground the way I drifted toward him. Sometimes I fell asleep with him in the fields after the ride even though I only wanted him to take me to his home.

In the mornings at his house as he dressed for work, I discovered the old *Charlie's Angels* that came on at six. I loved watching women with guns and hearing the sound of Charlie's friendly voice on the speaker box, the way he controlled everything without ever showing his face.

"Charlie's a good man," I made the mistake of telling Michael one day when I borrowed his gun without asking and posed in the lamplight to admire my silhouette on the living room walls.

He just looked at me.

My life was different once he knew how old I really was and wouldn't take me to bars anymore or let me leave his house in daylight.

———

Inside his living room, I'm gazing out the dusty windows. "Don't ask me why he won't let me watch television anymore," I say to my sisters on the phone, "because I won't tell you." My sisters are fascinated by television because my mother always refused to let us watch it. We never had a television at home, and our mother will probably never own one.

Mother isn't talking to me much anymore. Somehow I don't blame her. I wouldn't want to talk to me either, especially if I were her.

Michael bought me a walkie-talkie with a wide range and put the walkie-talkie in a little box on his desk so he could talk to me while he was away from his house. "Angel," he'll say on the speaker, "get ready for another mission." Then he'll ask me to do something I don't want to do like vacuum the stairs or take out the trash or clean the gutters. He likes to see what I can do with one bucket of soapy water and a sponge in the hours before he gets home from work.

It's easier walking through empty rooms, picking up Michael's cigarette stubs and trying on his ex-wife's tattered lingerie than leaving every morning to catch the bus to the high school. I hate biology and geometry, hate cutting up dead pigs and memorizing the equations for arcs and isosceles triangles. I'll never go back to being a student unless the sheriff will be my teacher as long as I live.

Three weeks ago was the last time. Mrs. Cummings, with her huge, fake blond hair, said I had a damaged mind. Dyslexic, she called me. I don't know if I was, but my eyes never wanted to move in straight lines. Goddamn my eyes! Reading forward and backwards, I got stuck in the middle of words I should have recognized, and I lost my place altogether. Whenever my teacher asked me to read aloud, I was terrified of what the other students would say about me. I tried to make them laugh, making up the words as I went along.

———

I'm an audio-visual learner. Michael used to say that the worst show on television is better than the greatest novel ever written, and he promised me that I'd never have to read again. But he couldn't cure my nightmares or my insomnia—not even the late, late shows could do that.

I don't know why Michael suddenly couldn't stand to see me watching *Charlie's Angels*. The actress with long dark hair that got tangled around her gun left a trail of dreams for me to follow along the highway. I had seen her shoot at men many times and miss, and her gun was too small to do much damage. Just the same, Michael must have been jealous of her. Maybe he thought I was in love with her, and maybe I was. I don't know for sure, but I think I once called out her name when he touched my hair in the night. *Jaclyn?* I just don't know.

———

During the day, I have Michael's house all to myself. The roof and its gutters are covered with cottonwood seeds. I hear leaves rustling over my head. The house is three stories high. Of twin balconies, only one remains, lapsing into decay, its floors and gates soft and grimy. The two windowed doors give me nightmares. One leads to a place of treetops, hummingbird feeders, locusts hovering. The other opens onto a three-story drop past the arched windows over the lumber stack.

I could step through the wrong door and fall towards trembling shadows over the woodpile. I could dive into the pond at the wood's edge, its brackish waters burning my eyes.

Flooded, again, the pond has encroached into the yard. Only the peaked roofs of the house and barn are visible below the treetops, their reflection wavering. Mallards roost on swollen shingles. Past cigarettes floating on the water, a gar swims deeper, gliding through the barn doors after writhing on the water's edge.

I want to walk under the pond, where everything is still, a wall lost to darkness. Even though I couldn't hear or see and might lose my sense of direction, unable to remember which way is up and which is down, I would remain calm, examining the cold metal of sunken cars. I want to reach through broken windows. I would be happy if the sheriff and I both swam under the water. Letting go of my breath, I would stroke his hair, his lips, his harsh, unshaven chin, even if he wouldn't respond to my touch.

I've never told him about my nightmares before. The pond is Michael's favorite place to go, and he would hate me for imagining us drowning in its waters, especially since the water has become my new obsession.

His old Mustang is his most valued possession. Three weeks ago, on his last drunken night, he almost drove into the water. Although he still calls me to ride with him and lets me sleep in his house, we haven't spoken ever since.

The Mustang rests on oversized tires. Michael paid to have its windows tinted and its sides detailed in airbrushed designs, a woman with enormous breasts cloaked in flames under a caption that reads *Light My Fire*.

I really don't blame the sheriff for loving his house and his car more than anything in the world. His parents died. His brothers and sisters married strangers and scattered, leaving him behind. They left the house and car with him.

"I hate this," he said that drunken night, tossing the green knitted blanket into the car window. "After all that money, they never did it right."

"What?' I asked.

"Her."

"Her?" I asked, pointing to the car.

"I gave the artist at the garage your picture from school. I said for her to look like you."

"Why?"

"They did it all wrong. Look at the mouth. Look at the eyes."

The sheriff searched his pants pocket for his keys, reaching for the longest one, then used its point to scrape the eyes away. He worked quickly, the paint flecks sticking to his fingers. "Fuck it," he said, smiling as he scratched away her lips. "I guess we just can't have nice things."

Now the airbrushed woman burns without a mouth, without eyes. She and I are the only women who remain near this house. Of all those who have lived here before me, I am the only one to stay without sisters, without a mother. Besides the sheriff, my only company is my shadow, my reflection in windows, long hazy mirrors, and family portraits.

Michael's family once made a living by breaking horses. It was a hard business, and in the photographs I can see the worry in his family's tired eyes.

In tarnished frames, thin gray women with light hair brush the hips of black stallions. A boy holding a rope reaches out to a cow skull. A tiny girl caresses a one-eyed kitten. A balding woman grips a dead turkey by its legs, the loose head dangling on the ground. All the men have sun-darkened faces. Distant, unsmiling, they stand in front of the house I know, holding rifles.

The youngest children, both male and female, are barefoot and clothed in the same rumpled long shirts that match the light tone of the cracked dirt around the porches, no pants to cover their legs. Someone, maybe Michael, has gone in with a faint pencil and written names under the feet—*Sarah, Haskell, Jo, Phillip, LeAnn.*

"Potato sacks," the sheriff called them, pointing to the long, shapeless shirts the children wore, whispering the words again and again as he looked away from the photographs and away from me to a place beyond the treetops outside the window.

His uncles suffered broken bones that wouldn't heal. In every family of horse-breakers, there comes a sign to stop breaking. There comes a time when the horses begin breaking the men instead of the men breaking the horses. His father was paralyzed in a hospital bed, and the mares were running wild, coming closer to the house until the women inside were scared to go outside. The horses fogged the windows with their hot breath before running to the highway to be shot down by local volunteers after stopping traffic. But there are no horses near the house now.

On the walls covered in mauve paper, rows of painted teal pears are barely visible behind the imprints of small hands. Once bleached by sunlight, they are dulled by evening, erased by nightfall. Silverfish dart and scatter, silent over their vines. Above the ceiling fan, the shadow of a single blade keeps turning while the house slowly falls apart.

———

Once when the television became too loud, more plaster chips fell away, and the sheriff ripped the cords out of the wall and threw the television into the trunk of his car, white dust clinging to his hairy arms.

The television used to soothe me, women telling me I deserve to change the color of my hair. I have had straight white-blond hair, brown curls, and jet-black braids held together by blue glass beads shaped like dolphins and lions, mermaids and tangerines.

On Channel 13, I once heard a man with a peppery beard say that television makes people lonely. He looked at the camera with his small gray eyes and said, "If you are watching right now and you think I am talking to you, then you have a problem." I never saw him again, but afterwards, I kept asking myself, what sort of problem? If he was saying "you," there had to be a "you," and since no one else was there, why couldn't "you" have been "me"?

———

I stay silent when I hear the front door open and close with a sigh. The sheriff's boots scrape the hall tiles. He calls my name before he walks into the living room, stinking of the gasoline he uses to wipe his hands. He is tall and slender with round glasses and a long, pointed nose. Although he is a heavy smoker, forty-nine years old, and not the type of man I had envisioned myself with, I suppose he is handsome, in his own way.

Michael taps a cigarette out of his shirt pocket and lights it before I realize he has struck the match. He holds the mark of a good man, the constant ability to surprise.

"Now," he says, touching the scratches made by knotted wood and metal rubbing against his arms, "you'll have to look at me. We'll have to start all over again, talking to each other." He holds the cigarette expertly in his thin lips, never touching it although the ash grows long and keeps bobbing with every word he speaks. "You're my little girl, aren't you?"

"No," I say, standing up to him so that our eyes are level. "I'm not little, not a girl."

"You're not?" the sheriff asks, taking in a deep drag, then slowly releasing the smoke, blowing into my face. I don't let him get to me. I'm careful not to frown, back away, or squint my eyes.

"I'm a woman."

The sheriff laughs and tries to kiss me while his chest rises and falls. I feel his stained teeth scraping against my mouth and try to pull away. We're nowhere near the same height, and he's stronger than I am. He grabs my wrist and twists my arm behind my back. I fall to my knees.

"What?" Michael asks, letting the ash drop on my hair. "I can't hear you?"

"Nothing," I say.

I lay down at his feet. He leans over me, stroking my back. "You're my little baby-angel girl," he says, "and always will be."

His lips graze my neck. I put my arms around his waist. He leans back, the crown of his head resting against my chin. His hair smells of tobacco and earth rotting under tree shadow. With my polished nails, I unknot his tangles, mussing up the dark strands, imagining his badge in my hand, the way it would warm in my fingers.

Michael sighs, lighting one cigarette with another. He holds still for me while I ruffle his hair, searching for the white of his scalp. I wonder how long before he goes gray like his daddy in the photos, bald like his grandpa. He is strong now with muscled arms, but I need to know if he will still be strong in twenty years. I wonder if there was ever a horse that could have broken him like his father was broken. I never want to see a man that way. I left my sisters and my mother to be with the sheriff, and my mother fears I will stay with him forever, living as his wife, even if only by common law.

"Nice hair," I say, trying to make my voice sound dusky, older.

"You're the creepiest girl I know."

The sheriff turns around to me, flicking his ash under the rug. I touch my mouth to his wrists and begin to kiss his hands. Michael tastes of salt and ashes, beer and burning leaves, good flavors that tell me he works hard even during summer evenings.

———

When the sheriff lies on top of me and falls asleep, I remain awake.

"You're going," he says if I wake him by shifting beneath his body. In my mind, I'm already gone. "I want you to stay. Just the same, you're gone."

"When?"

Tomorrow I could be back in my mother's house with the music, bumping into my sisters in the halls. But I know if Michael and I fall asleep in each other's arms we will be less likely to let go of each other in the morning.

"What are you doing?" he asks.

"Nothing . . . thinking."

When I was a little girl, I used to feel sorry for dead butterflies and for my father. "Dad is dead," my mother used to say to my sisters and me. Then the flood washed through the cemetery. "Mother told a lie," she whispered, her bare feet sinking into the soaked ground.

My father was born on an Indiana farm in springtime, the oval pond iced over, broken windows floating on gasoline. The white-gray geese were simply gone. The flock left without warning, never to return. His sister's scarves were rising to the pond's surface, the leather gloves crushed and faded like wilted violets swirling through spilled oil and lipstick-stained cigarettes. He would not talk for years, would not look at a woman's hands, and then he spoke to his sister only in dreams, decades later when he was married to my mother and I was his baby girl. Holding his hand in the dark, I watched Pia stand beside the cradle she rocked even in her sleep.

"Someone's lying," he would say. His hand was too big for my hand. In the bath, he would fit both of my hands and my feet in his hand to keep me warm in the water. His finger and thumb closed over my ankles, his eyes moving rapidly under their lids.

Mother sat shivering in a chair near the open window, her hands over her chest as she stared out at the trees.

"Don't look at his eyes," she said.

"Daddy?" I say without meaning to say it.

All night, beneath the sheriff in the stillness under the shattered window, while he sleeps, I dance without moving to songs he never hears. In the silence, I somehow learn to hold him like I once held my father, without disturbing his dreams.

———

As Michael wakes, he and I just stare at each other's mouth, keeping quiet, and breathing softly in time as if we were prisoners in his house. Gazing at his thin lips, I wonder if in taking what I wanted I've somehow given too much of myself away.

I love his house's high windows and its closeness to water and its dampness, the stench of his old cigarettes. I want to sleep here more than any place in the world. Even during my insomnia attacks, I know better than to tell Michael that I want to remain. If I did, he would think I want him to marry me and would probably want me to go away. So I pretend every night is the last, keeping my lipsticks and curlers in their boxes.

I stand on my tiptoes and put my hands on his shoulders. He yawns, and I follow him down the hall to his room.

"Scooch over," the sheriff says when I finally climb into his bed. He reaches for a blanket draped over the quilt rack. The blanket is made of green yarn, knotted and torn by my fingers that have caught and tangled in the threads.

"Why do you have to tear things up?" he asks, gazing through the holes. "You've ruined so many nice things."

"I'm sorry," I say, although I have no idea what I've ruined besides the blanket. Then I start to walk around the house while he waits, and I see all the broken mirrors and shattered windows as if for the first time, realizing what I've done.

"Why?" is a question we never ask each other.

I ripped the blanket four nights ago. I didn't even know what I was doing when I tore into the yarn. I was lying underneath Michael. He wouldn't let me touch him, and I needed something to hold on to.

———

The sheriff doesn't talk much at night. There's nothing to say anymore. I usually wait for him to go to sleep so I can quietly slip away. Mostly, I only traipse the rooms above, my high heels clomping on the hardwood floors. I imagine I'm invisible, not even a reflection in the window.

My voice whispers to itself before my skinny legs in the mirror startle me and I stumble down the stairs. I hate the mirrors in his house as the reflections that they cast seem untrue—an awkward girl in women's clothes so large they swallow her body, slipping off her hips and shoulders. Where did his ex-wife go in such a hurry that she didn't need to pack any of her clothes?

I lean out the open windows near the high tree branches

and look for new locusts, wet and green. I put them in glass jars then watch them escaping their shells. They are fragile and smell faintly of summer rain and leaves. I watch their filmy eyes harden and turn dark like amber glass. Their wings unfold as they dry into inky veins. When I open the jars, the locusts take flight. Later, I reach for the brown husks and drop them, watching as they spiral slowly down—brittle, hollow, dull, and lost to darkness.

Sometimes I sing to the new locusts in a whisper, wondering if Michael can hear me and if insects recognize my song. Whenever I dream of horses running from our shadows, I want to tell the sheriff, but I'm afraid of what he might say. I want to write the story of his life and mine, but I can't write well. I only sit down with paper and pens and realize nothing interesting has ever happened to me besides him. The horses are just a second-hand memory, and the locusts are the only miracle I've ever known.

Allison's Idea

In late September, the monarchs flew away. I wanted to paint them. Instead, I rode in Kathy's blue convertible and winced each time their orange and black wings burst on the windshield. As she drove, she adjusted the radio and asked what I wanted for lunch. I finally understood her: she couldn't feel pain in wings she didn't have.

Because she was driving, it couldn't have been my fault.

Our destination, Melissa's house, was our favorite meeting place as children. The five of us—Kathy, Melissa, Rachel, Allison, and me—used to congregate in the front lawn under the maples. Around roots thicker than our arms, we dug holes with rusted shovels. Then we filled the pits with water and stirred, pretending to make witches' brew. The rest of us tossed in weeds and pinecones, but Rachel insisted on sacrifices. After capturing mantises, crickets, and grasshoppers, she decapitated them, then tore off their legs and cast the pieces in. The precision of her killing amazed me, and now she wants to be a surgeon.

Under the maples, the five of us had one dream, to live together and grow very long hair. Nothing changed. First, we were girls dreaming women's dreams. Then we were women remembering our childhood. All I wanted was to see those maples again. I thought one glimpse of their height and the shadow lands under their leaves would convince me a little magic from our childhood survived.

"Melissa wants to cut her hair," Kathy said. I looked at the strawberry-blond curls cascading past Kathy's shoulders.

"Why on Earth?" I asked.

"Don't ask me. Hers is the longest. I would die to have it."

"I won't let her."

"Don't worry," she said, "neither will I."

We came to the old neighborhood and pulled into the driveway where the cul-de-sac ended. "We're here," she said.

"No," I said.

The maples were dying, their leaves lost in webs tent worms spun as they devoured. Dead leaves crumbled under the force of wind and insects dancing. Black-faced worms gyrated, their furry bodies slinking and rising. Their webs were held together by a syrupy residue just as filth will bond human hair. No one had bothered to stop them from spreading.

"I can't believe this," I said.

"Why not? This has been the worst season. Everything is dying," Kathy said.

"How could Melissa let it happen?"

"It wasn't her fault."

"Then whose fault was it?" I asked. She didn't answer.

The wind rose up, and a monarch flew into my scattered hair. I flicked it away and pulled the hair out of my eyes.

"Why did you kill that butterfly?" Kathy asked.

"I didn't," I said as I wiped the dull pollen off my fingers and onto my jeans. Then I looked down at the driveway and saw the monarch flapping its wings and its body going nowhere.

Rachel ran out onto the lawn with Melissa close behind her. When the four of us hugged, our hair tangled together. When we separated, we were still pulling strands out of our eyes. We looked at the dying maples for the last time and couldn't leave fast enough.

We formed a caravan to the house Allison's father had bought for us. It was close to campus, and Allison waited for us there. The house was newly decorated in pink and green, more than large enough for the five of us, and equipped with picture windows, a columnar porch, and bare walls to hang my paintings on.

"I saved the best room for you," Allison said, and she had. There was so much natural light pouring in that I converted it into a studio right away.

The neighbors' children welcomed us after we settled into our new home. They brought casseroles their mothers had baked, and Allison wanted to give them something in return. She broke out a package of store-bought chocolate-chip cookies but couldn't decide what to serve them on. Her first thought was the children might break her new dishes. Her second was that if she served the cookies in a dog-food bowl no one would notice.

But I did. Knowing what Allison had done, how could I blame myself? The cookie incident above all others assured me it wasn't my fault.

———

We were lonely. Our beautiful house was spacious, empty. Our families were far away from us. At first, we cleaned the house until it gave off a white, sterile glow, but all that work was just affection wasted on glass cleaner and furniture polish. The windows could only shine so much. We needed something to take care of, something to call our own. I don't know who first mentioned we should adopt pets. Looking back, I believe it was probably Allison's idea. I know it wasn't mine.

I hated animals, the smell of wet fur, fleas, jagged teeth that bite. But now I believe lonely women are the most dangerous creatures. After what we've been through, I should know.

"Dogs and cats? No, no, just think what they'll do," I said. "They'll tear this house apart."

"What else is there?" Melissa asked.

"Plants," I said, "they clean the air. They take in the sun and won't bark or bite or pee on the carpet."

"I want a puppy," Allison said.

"Our new mauve carpet," I said.

I filled our windowsills with foliage of all kinds: rubber plants, parrot plants, pink splashes, daisies. Any leafy creature that required indirect light and matched our color scheme would do. The plants made the house come alive. They breathed. They rustled. They took only sun from the windows and water from a pail, and they survived.

I was particularly fond of my red daisy. When it grew its first bud, I suddenly understood what Redon saw when he drew *A Flower with a Child's Face*. On instinct, I almost took the daisy with me.

But when it came time for vacation, I had places to go. Melissa and Rachel stayed home.

"We'll water the plants for you," Melissa said.

When I came back a week later, all the plants were dead. My daisy's stem was twisted. The leaves were withered. The roots were black. The tiny face of the bud, looking up to sun when I left, now looked to the soil.

"Over here," I said to Rachel while holding the dead flower over the trash.

"What?" she asked, barely turning away from the television.

I touched my finger to the bud. "A child, head down, crying," I said then dropped it into the wastebasket.

"Oh, I didn't know how to tell you. We forgot to water," Melissa said.

"They bored us so much we let them die," Rachel said.

Next Allison bought blue-green fish that looked pink and metallic when they caught the light. They were beautiful but would kill one another if they lived together in the same bowl. Allison eventually refused to change their water. Rachel thought the fish were stupid—always still, never dancing. I wasn't surprised the night Melissa went out to dump them into a pond. Only the determined look on her face frightened me. Later, she told me she thought the fish would survive.

Then my friends, mourning their wasted affections, sought out colorful birds. At first, I was impressed. They even taught their birds to say a few phrases, but Allison was frustrated because her parrot couldn't say her name. When it eventually said "Melissa," she was furious. Later, the birds proved to be tedious by nature—hollow bones, tiny brains. As Rachel put it, "never strong enough to truly love you."

I watched in amusement when Melissa went out to the backyard to "set the birds free." Their wings were clipped and they couldn't fly, but this didn't stop her from trying. She opened the cage doors but couldn't understand why the birds didn't rush out. Just as Melissa was about to give up, Rachel ran out to help her. One by one, she tossed the birds up into the air. They tried to fly but found themselves stranded on tree branches.

"Why don't you just give them away?" I shouted out the window.

They loaded the birds into Kathy's car and went from door to door. But no one would take them.

Finally, Kathy said, "I'll take care of them."

I kept wondering what she did with them. Suddenly, they just disappeared, cages and all. About a week later, I heard a strange sound coming from the basement. The light wouldn't come on. So in the dark, I walked down the concrete steps and found the birds at the bottom—starving, starving. The sound? Wings beating on the cages, shrill cries, bird songs. But I'll never forget the voice of Allison's parrot calling, "Melissa, Melissa . . ." over and over and over again.

I don't know how long I stayed at the bottom of the dark basement listening. I just remember Kathy coming down to lead me away. When we reached the top of the stairs, it was morning.

"Don't worry. I'll take care of it," she said. After that, the birds truly did disappear.

———

Late one evening, the five of us stayed up talking about plants, fish, cats, dogs, and birds. We lingered on death, but no one mentioned murder.

"You realize none of this was my fault?" I asked.

"Who said it was?" Allison asked.

Somewhere between night and morning, we decided that children were really the ideal thing—cuddly, affectionate, able to whisper and shout, so responsive to their own names, so in need of love; in short, so human. But we were much too young and carefree to consider motherhood, or so we thought. (Our friends who already had children had just that—children and nothing else.)

We thought the logical move would be to look for pets more like ourselves. The more human characteristics a creature had, the more valuable it was to us. But that was the trouble. Not even the most expensive, most discriminating pet shops carried animals with the intelligence and sensitivity we desired.

Soon we found other markets. Or rather, they found us when we took out loans, mortgaged our vehicles, signed up for more credit cards.

———

We drove to exotic-animal farms where we met skinny men with gleaming eyes and amazing suntans. No one bothered to ask questions. We just looked through cages at beautiful creatures that smelled of death. When we found an animal we adored, the men named their price and flashed gold-toothed smiles. We paid and paid them, placing crumpled bills in their dusty palms. Then we drove away, hoping our precious creatures would survive the journey home.

But even after visiting the last exotic-animal farm, Kathy found nothing that pleased her.

Melissa acquired a giant yellow bird with green tail feathers and brown eyes framed by what looked like a woman's lashes brushed with mascara. She said the bird winked at her, and she couldn't resist. It had an amazing vocabulary when she bought it. Although its words rarely made sense, she planned to teach it a song.

Rachel had purchased a miniature, melon-colored frog. The smiling men made her promise never to take it out of the jar because its skin leaked poison. But she wanted to hold it anyway because its front legs ended in what looked like the soft ivory fingers of an infant.

"Oh, don't do it, Rachel. You really shouldn't," Kathy said to her.

"Don't do it. Don't do it," Melissa's bird chanted.

Every now and then, the tiny, blue-eyed frog stretched its baby fingers. Rachel cooed at it all the way home, but by the time we pulled into the driveway it was dead.

Allison's white monkey Peeper was the most expensive purchase, the most willful animal, and the hardest to control. We all wanted him, but Allison was the only one who could afford him. Peeper was worth the money because he was childlike. His tail ended in a black tip that matched the color of his eyes. Every now and then, he covered those eyes with hands that looked so human I wanted to hold them. But he refused to stand still long enough for us to catch him. Like a naughty little boy, he tied our hair in knots. The very first night he spent at our house, he crawled out an open window. We never saw him again.

———

I wasn't going to buy anything, but as we were leaving the last exotic-animal farm one of the men unloaded a plant with long, fine red petals swaying. The delicate petals reminded me of a woman's hair tossed by the wind. The men called it a sensitive plant. The leaves were arranged in patterns of five. When I touched them, they wrapped around one of my fingers like a gossamer fist closing. The yellow center of the petals was spotted blue and brown. The colors made a design that looked like lips and eyes. A woman-flower, maybe its peaceful face was just an illusion of color patterns, but it was more than I had hoped for.

We spent many pleasant mornings on our porch. Melissa showed off her bird, obediently sitting on her shoulder and singing "Silent Night." But once when a bobwhite cried out from the trees, the golden bird beat its wings so rapidly that Melissa's lips bled. She screamed, and I'll never forget the shadow her giant bird cast as it flew away from her.

———

Our final journey to replace our lost pets was different from our previous journeys. An anonymous caller told Allison about a seller who had discovered a new breed. For the first time, we traveled toward one man and no exotic farm.

On a street littered with papers and soda bottles, he introduced himself. His right hand shielded his lips as he spoke.

"I'm a breeder," he said, his voiced hurried. "I'll show you something. What I've got."

"Maybe some other time," I said.

"Now, now listen up. Now, here's something you won't see every day," he said.

"Oh, we might as well. Just to see what he has," Allison said. "We've already come all this way. There's really nothing left to lose."

When he looked at us, I imagined what he saw—designer clothes. The five of us were full of our parents' money, strutting down the streets of a strange and crowded city. He was leading us into the poorer neighborhoods. We were ready for adventure, ready to believe anything that got us what we wanted. I caught no mockery in anything he said, no treachery in his blue eyes appraising. When he spoke, he whispered nervously. Only the left half of his mouth was moving.

Outside a small house, I watched as the old man led my friends away. Melissa occasionally looked back at me, and I feared for her safe return. But there was no reasoning, nothing I could do to stop them.

———

When it came time, Allison was not waiting in the front as she had promised. So, I reached into my purse and grabbed my pearl-handled nail file as if it could save us all. I knocked on the apartment door. When no one answered, I let myself in. I heard a scream below me and ran down a concrete staircase to find out where the scream had come from. Clutching my nail file tight, I stumbled and almost fell several times. I could hear animals whimpering and smell their terror. When

I reached the bottom of the staircase, I saw Rachel laughing and holding her checkbook. The breeder was beside her.

"No checks. No use for them here," he said to her.

"So how do I pay you? We want those baby doggies. Oh please, can we take them to a good home. But I don't have much cash on me," Rachel said.

"I'll take the cash," he said. "Nothing else. Maybe your rings. Maybe her watch. Maybe your car—no checks."

"He can't have the car," I said.

"We'll talk later," Rachel said through clenched teeth. Turning to the old man, she said, "What's it going to be?"

"What do you have on you?" he asked.

"You're both insane!" I shouted to Rachel. But she carelessly waved a hand in my direction dismissing my words as I uttered them.

The smell of animals grew stronger with the smell of urine, the smell of rot, the smell of neglect. What did Rachel say to the old man, "baby doggies"? "Doggies?" We already tried "doggies." We didn't like them. I thought we had moved on to more interesting creatures. However, I was curious to find out what new breed my friends had so madly fallen in love with.

One by one, Rachel pulled her rings off with considerable effort. She tried to be swift about the deed but couldn't. A silver ring with a large purple stone caught on her right hand's middle finger. She was still attempting to loosen it when I ran into the next room where Allison, Kathy, and Melissa were saying, "Oh, oh, come here!" They went on, not realizing I was there.

"Oh, look at it! Isn't it cute?"

"Sweet little things."

"Come here! Come here!"

"Oh, I've never seen anything like them. Precious. Just precious."

I went deeper into the little room that was just concrete floors, concrete walls, concrete ceilings, neon lights buzzing, no windows. But I still couldn't see the animals. Allison, Kathy, and Melissa were crowded around them in a half-circle of admiration. The animals were apparently backed up against the wall.

"Oh, they're perfect, perfect."

"Are you hungry, sweetheart? Are you hungry? Well, here you go."

"Melissa, we don't even know what to feed them. He hasn't told us yet. Melissa!"

"Oh, look, he likes it. Look, look, she wants one, too."

"Oh, let me give her one. Let me give it to her. Over here, honey. Over here!"

"Good girl. Good girl!"

When I broke through their little circle, nothing could have prepared me for what I saw. The animal they fed was no dog. It was a little blonde-haired girl. She had blue eyes and must have been only three or four years old. Her clothes were rags. Allison tried to give her more food, but she was too shy to take it. So, Allison put it on the floor beside her, and she grabbed it up. Such a lithe creature! She turned away from us and hid her face in the wall as she devoured scraps not fit for a dog. Then she turned back around for more. Her eyes met mine and she crawled toward me.

"What's happened to her? Someone help me get her off the floor," I said.

Then the old man came in.

"These are children," I said.

He just looked at me.

"No, no, these are doggies," Melissa said.

The breeder, still looking at me, said, "You are both right. These are dog-children. The first and the last of their kind."

I'm not the one who believed him, but I allowed my friends to purchase the boy and the girl. At that moment, my only intention was to get them out of the filth. Determined to have no part in my friends' madness, I ignored the children. But during the ride home, the little girl would sit only with me. She ignored Melissa. She whimpered when Rachel touched her. She ran from Allison. She flinched when Kathy patted her head and refused the company of her brother.

We didn't even bother to name them. From the first, they were just "the boy" and "the girl." I never cared for the boy. He was the wild one, knocking over chairs, begging for our dinners, licking our hands. My friends adored him. However, they were disappointed by the girl. Rachel complained she was too calm, too quiet.

"Why does she want only you?" Kathy asked me. I couldn't tell her why.

For six months, I watched the news to listen for kidnappings. No child lost or stolen fit the description of our dog-children. And they became more like animals every day. I began to think maybe the old man had accomplished something amazing. The dog-children could do things normal children couldn't. Nothing could account for their instincts and speed. They had the ability to hear sounds long before we could. And the things normal children could do, they couldn't—for instance, speaking, reasoning, understanding. And to my surprise they grew much faster than children. Isn't one year to a human the same as seven to a dog? Maybe they grew so fast because we fed them and when we found them they were starving, starving.

From the beginning, I knew the girl was a better creature than the boy. If I left my paintbrushes scattered on the floor, she straightened them in a line. My exotic flower fascinated her. She touched its stems and blew on its petals. The leaves grasped her slender fingers. However, she understood not to touch the plant without my consent.

One evening, she watched me paint. I dropped my palette on the floor, and she handed the palette back to me. When I looked down at her, she was using the spilled paint to color her own picture. The image looked like trees, rainbows, stars, and smiling faces. From that moment on, I knew I had to protect the girl.

At night she and I sat alone in my room. I tried to teach her to speak. I said short words like "sun" or "star" over and over again. She watched attentively then moved her lips, but no words came out. Walking was more difficult. I pulled her up under her shoulders, and she moved her legs. But she couldn't support herself because her legs were twisted from crawling and wouldn't straighten.

Every now and then Rachel came into the room and said, "Teaching your dog tricks again? The boy can leap over the sofa and roll down the stairs in a ball. What can she do? We should have left her where we found her."

One night Allison and I left the dog-children alone so we could walk at the park. We admired the city lights reflecting on the pond's still surface. We waded out into the waters up to our ankles but were afraid to go deeper because the black waters mirrored the night sky and we couldn't see our toes. Then we heard a sound like a wounded animal making its way through the fallen leaves. The sound became louder. The animal moved closer. We put our shoes on without tying the laces and ran toward the car. We were halfway there when we found the boy sitting in the middle of our path. I couldn't stand to look at him. Allison tried to comb the hair out of his eyes, but he was in no mood for affection. He clawed her arms with the sharp nails he refused to let us trim.

We were silent on the way home. Of course, we both knew what it meant. The park was at least a mile away from the house, and the boy had tracked us there.

———

At home we found the girl whimpering under the kitchen table. The boy ran circles and circles around the living room. The food bowls were empty, and I went to fill them. Allison stopped me and said, "No, we have to punish them."

"Them?" I asked.

"Them."

"But the girl, what did she do?"

"That's not the point," Allison said, hurling the empty bowl at the running boy. The bowl hit him on the ear, and he turned around. He moved toward Allison. She took a step back behind me and closed her eyes. The room was silent until the girl broke the awkward moment by howling. Allison chased the girl and the boy into the dark basement.

Later that night, Allison and I approached Rachel, but she wouldn't believe us.

"Oh, he must have been in the back of the car," she said.

"You think we just imagined it?" Allison asked.

"Well, next time lock the doors," Kathy said.

"He tore through the screen," I said.

———

From then on, we never opened the windows, and whenever I left the house the girl stood in my studio doorway. At first, I thought she was waiting for me. Then I realized she was guarding the door. If no one was watching, the boy ran for the sensitive plant. The girl did her best to keep him away from it.

For the first time in our lives, we knew fear. My friends no longer liked the boy. He bit them. His teeth were like razors slipping on their legs or shattered glass penetrating their fingers.

Everything changed the night he bit me. I was eating french fries and watching television. Occasionally, I gave the girl a piece of my dinner. I didn't feed her because she reminded me of a desperate animal. Rather, I fed her because she never begged.

The boy was different. He whimpered, pawed, and ran circles around me. I couldn't forgive him for disturbing my dinner. So, every time he came near, I pushed him away from my plate.

The last time I decided to push him harder. I heard his neck pop. Then he growled and sunk his teeth into my hand. I screamed for him to let go. He wouldn't. I called to Rachel, Allison, Melissa, and Kathy to help me. They didn't. When I saw my torn skin hanging and the blood seeping out from his mouth, I decided the boy and the girl weren't human. Suddenly, the old man was eccentric but a genius. We were the saviors, taking two freakish creatures away from certain death in the outside world where doctors would dissect them.

The girl ran to me, but I found no comfort in her affections. I put my hand in cold water then walked to my studio to paint my flower. The girl must have been close behind me, but I didn't hear her. The boy must have followed her, but I didn't know he lurked in the dark hallway.

I stared at my exotic flower. It grew more beautiful, more feminine every day. I touched the leaves, and they held my finger. How could this plant be so human while the children outside my door were more animals than people? For a moment, I thought the flower smiled, but I must have been dreaming.

Dreaming, because I was awakened by a growl. There was a pounding on the door, and suddenly it was off its hinges. The boy came in and flashed a toothy grin. The girl jumped on his back and grabbed onto his face. The next thing I knew, her fingers were in his mouth, and she was screaming.

I ran toward her, but the look on her face told me she wanted me to stay away. The boy lunged toward me. The girl tried to hold him back. He was stronger than she, and she failed.

He ran at me, I dodged him, and he crashed into my flower. The daisy hit the floor. Its face and petals were decapitated from the stem. The leaves clinched then relaxed.

I didn't even feel the boy's teeth going into my hand. He bit me again and then scurried away on all fours. The girl remained, weeping for my flower, she sat at my feet.

"Get out," I said. "Get out of here!"

She didn't budge.

"I hate animals—the smell of wet fur, fleas, jagged teeth that bite," I said as I kicked her away from me.

"I never bit you," she said.

I begged her to repeat it, but she only barked, whimpered, and rolled over and over as if she never had spoken at all. Then she looked at me with her blue eyes, the eyes of that breeder.

I found Rachel and said, "He sold his children."

My friends tried to convince me I was wrong.

"Look at him. You call him human?" Rachel asked, pointing to the boy.

"I really can't believe he murdered your beautiful flower," Melissa said.

"The girl?" Kathy said. "If she was human, she would have talked by now."

"Why don't they talk?" Rachel asked. "Why don't they understand what we're saying? Why does he bite us?"

"I'll tell you why," Allison said. "They're not even human beings. That's why."

I heard the dog-children howling and the voices of Allison, Rachel, Kathy, and Melissa convincing me it was also my fault. They kept saying I was wrong, that the girl and the boy were never children. But I knew. I knew.

"I'll take care of them," Kathy whispered.

"I'll come with you," Rachel said.

"Don't do it," I said, pleading. But there was no reasoning, no way to stop them.

Allison held me back, her fingernails clawing my arms.

Rachel and Kathy led the dog-children out of the house and into the backyard. The floodlights went out, and from my side of the window I heard the girl's voice pleading.

"I never bit you. I never bit you," she said.

"Did she say something?" Kathy asked.

"No," Rachel said, "not a thing."

"I never . . ."

"But I thought I heard something," Kathy said.

"It must have been me," Rachel said.

"Never . . ."

By then, not even I was listening. The lights in the neighbors' houses were coming on. Sirens were howling in the distance. The neighbors' children were pressed against their bedroom windows and scratching on the glass like animals wanting to escape the houses they always come back to.

SHRIKE

Women in distant neighborhoods raked burnt shingles like fallen leaves from their front yards. Occasionally, a woman would find a beautiful relic, some piece of painted mural that had traveled on the wind to the houses, a singed mermaid, the green tail of pinkish scales studded with glass shards as bright as crushed diamonds, a charred ballerina with no legs, night sky spattered with white, glittering stars that shed paint flecks like rust when touched by even the gentlest hand.

A few people began collecting remnants, paying a small price for each fragment large enough to be framed under glass. I grew to know these collectors as well as my mother, who was one of them. Searching for fragments pertaining to old movie stars of the forties and fifties, she and I walked the vacant lots littered with the cinema's fragile remains.

I was embarrassed when Mother hired the few teenagers who were still my friends to scavenge the surrounding areas with her. In my high school years, I was constantly hiding from kids my age, comfortable only when watching them from a safe distance. Kristen Rue tolerated me because she said I was so quiet that sometimes she felt like being with me was like being alone. Zach Corson, the college boy who drove his Mustang across fields the way my grandfather used to ride horses, had mercy on me and gave me a lot of advice back then. He said if I dyed my hair red and spoke a different language some of the weird kids would start to notice me and take pity on me. Until then, he would teach me the ways of the world, including how small and smelly the world was when he put his arm around me and my nose was crushed against his armpit.

That day when the teenagers were searching without me and Zach was hugging me too hard, I wanted him to drive off the field and put Kristen and the fire behind us, but Mother's hobby was bringing us together and making too many people remember.

While Zach held me tight inside his car, Mother occasionally beckoned to us. I can still see her ironic smile as she approached the Mustang from time to time and asked me to join the search. I watched the boys' quick, awkward hands as they combed the fields while racing against the coming rain. Kristen dove down into the brush with my mother, delicate shreds of vintage posters scattered through the high, dry grasses.

While I tried to make conversation with Zach, to get him to talk about anything but the fire, I realized he wasn't listening to me. He was watching Kristen. He had eyes for only her. His head bobbed up and down every time she bobbed at the field's edge, reaching through the low branches above her head and then to the fallen branches at her feet to remove fragments caught in the leaves. While she filled her satchel with scorched prints, I turned up the radio and whispered. The station was playing The Beach Boys "Wouldn't It Be Nice." For some reason, that song always made me sad. I guess even then I had this feeling that "it" wouldn't be nice, whatever it was. So, I turned up the radio to maximum volume and whispered again, "Please, Zach, no." For some reason, I didn't want to hear my own voice when I spoke to him.

———

That evening when the old cinema burnt down on Green Street, I had seen the smoke rising and thought of theater screens smoldering to black ash. The sky disappeared past Duck Street, near Charlotte Avenue where sparks rose on wind, drifting over rooftops. Ash fell like snow in the northeast, dusting the hair of every head in the crowd that had begun to circle the ambulance where Christopher, Libby Sortie's child, was being tended to behind closed doors.

As the ashes drifted away, I tried not to think of winter in upstate New York. I had spent my early childhood there before my family moved to Oklahoma. After that move, my father gave us new names again and we tried to escape the collection agencies. That year he chose our names from a small book about songbirds of the western trailside. Mother was Catbird Bushtit, which Father shortened to Cat. Father chose the name Wilson Warbler.

For reasons that are now beyond my comprehension, I begged to be called Loggerhead Shrike, but Father said, "No, absolutely not. And, if you don't shut up about it, you'll be known as Williamson's Sapsucker until you're old enough to vote."

Maybe I thought Loggerhead was the name of a girl who no one would ever want to rub the wrong way. I just couldn't imagine any neighborhood bully calling out,

"Hey, Loggerhead, come here and get your head handed to you." That name "Loggerhead" was too damn fearsome. No one would dare think of handing Loggerhead's head to her on a silver platter. Her name was the calling card of a girl the other kids wouldn't want to piss off. Loggerhead Shrike meant business. Even her last name had a nice ring to it. I could hear the new principal taking stock of my name, getting a good first impression and knowing I couldn't be intimidated. If I arrived late to school and he caught me sneaking in, he would have to say, "Well, well, Miss Shrike, what do you have to say for yourself?" Or, Mother, upon getting the detention slip would say, "God damn it, Loggerhead!"

Despite my schemes, none of that ever happened because, eventually, Father and I compromised on my new name, Veery Thrush. But Mother ran the household and had the final say when it came to every decision, even names. Laughing at us, she threw the bird book into the wastebasket and chose names from the air: Peter, Jane, and Sara Smith.

"All right, Cat, if that's the way you want it," Father said. "But Veery and I are a little disappointed by your selections. Aren't we, Veery?"

Neither of them gave me a chance to answer. I kept my mouth shut when they argued.

"Who ever heard of a woman named Catbird Bushtit?" Mother asked, lighting another cigarette. "Catbird Bullshit is more like it. You think any of the new neighbors would want to invite me over for coffee with a name like that? And why wouldn't the three of us have the same last name?"

"Lots of reasons," Father said, plunking a few ice cubes into his cranberry juice and vodka.

"For God's sakes, Darrel. What would a Wilson Warbler be doing living with a Catbird Bushtit and raising a child named Veery Thrush? Did you ever think of that?"

"Your mother has a point there, Sara," Father said, taking the bird book out of the wastebasket and brushing it off on his sleeve.

"Thank you, Peter," Mother said, pulling down the blinds.

———

Even the cinema fire reminded me of that other life and the lost names that slipped away from us like the people we abandoned without warning—something long ago, my mother crying into a red-silk pillow as Father's hands moved softly against the blond-brick walls of the house he had built, the house we had to leave behind.

Maybe because southern Oklahoma hadn't had a decent snowfall in years, the children laughed with their hands held high as the dark smoke choked the blue out of the sky. Even the grass and the leaves were dusted with whitish-gray flakes. Children ran around the adults. Men's legs opened like doors for toddlers to swagger through. Small, smudged hands scissored across the wind before the children came together in secretive pairs to compare the ash on one palm to the ash on another.

Everyone except me seemed to ignore the children. The mothers trusted me too much. The fathers smiled and looked away, as if they assumed their children were safe because I wasn't ashamed to be near them and because I didn't cry out whenever one of them bit me. The children screamed for joy as the wind rose, lifting fragments of the cinema's roof into the air. I held the smaller children from time to time, spinning them, lifting them over my shoulders. Thin, wispy shreds of the burnt cinema soared beyond the treetops, curtain threads tangling, speeding up and slowing down, zigzagging on air like feathers across the surface of a stormy pond.

Since the local reporters were already on scene, interviewing the fire chief in front of the truck, I was worried Kristen would be filmed while standing in the background. I wanted to hide behind the pecan trees, but I knew that hiding would only attract more attention. Caught between my desire to hear what the men were saying and my desire to remain out of view, I tried to listen just out of camera range, my back to the reporters. As I looked casually behind me, I shifted position ever so slightly whenever I saw a camera moving.

Chief Williams seemed to be looking in my direction, but I was sure it was just my imagination. I had always trusted him, believing he was a dependable, intelligent man, but he knew too much. He wasn't looking at the reporters, but farther away in Kristen's direction while he spoke. He claimed it was a difficult decision, but a necessary one—to let the cinema burn to the ground rather than risk the lives of firefighters to save the old building that was already halfway gone with no one now left inside. Apparently, because there was so little rain that August when Christopher Sortie was burned, the firemen's priority was to make sure the fire died where it started so that none of the nearby buildings would catch. Firemen were standing outside the cinema, aiming their hoses at the high broken windows and into holes in the open roof.

People in the crowd were still gathering, shouting Christopher's name before they followed him and his mother and the paramedics to the ambulance.

Kristen remained silent.

Zach rushed from behind the liquor store with a garden hose in hand, aiming the water at the roof of his grandfather's hardware store. If a single spark drifted on the wind to the old wooden shingles, the roof would go up in an instant. Kristen looked away as he caught her eye, and I realized how quickly his family business could be lost. Suddenly, I wanted to see him seeing it burn.

My father was telling my mother that Christopher would probably be fire chief one day. I couldn't bear to hear it, even though I knew the boy would be pleased with what had happened. He was a hero already, and not just in his own mind. Even though he was only eleven years old, he had risked his life to save another, having gone into the flames before the firemen arrived to rescue an alley cat and returning with a little girl in his arms.

The girl, Tina Borne, was unscathed. She danced to music that played on her wind-up lullaby glow-worm doll, the tips of her slippers just singed where the blackened ribbon touched asphalt.

Christopher was not so fortunate. His hair and eyelashes had been burnt away. His eyebrows were gone, and even when he was out of the building he inhaled like a boy who had been holding his breath too long while swimming underwater. He had descended the steps of the cinema with Tina's face covered by his shirt, and my mother began to scream. Just as Christopher set Tina down under the shade of the oak trees, Tina uncovered her face, tossed the shirt to the ground, and held her doll up in the air. The lullaby began to play, the delicate tinkling song like rain on antique glass. Kristen ran to him. Christopher staggered to her like a drunken man before he fell face first into the grass, his face at her boots. He made no attempt to rise.

As I approached him, I was surprised scorched skin glistened angrily where his soft curls had once fallen into his eyes. I held him in a wooden way, careful not to let anything touch his head where the hair and skin had been replaced by blisters and red wounds.

"Mommy," he whispered, the silver lighter falling out of his hand.

"I'm not your mother," I whispered back, slipping the lighter into his jacket pocket when I was sure no one else was looking.

Kristen was crying then.

Steadying Christopher while we waited for the paramedics, I knew Kristen blamed herself. Libby had asked her to watch him, to keep him clear of disaster. But disaster came to him more often than it came to other little boys she had babysat over the years.

"The flames are alive," Christopher had once told me when he found Kristen and me sitting alone at the diner where his mother worked. I'm sure he thought no one else could hear him. "They know me. I'm the one who feeds them after they're born."

Kristen just looked at me and wiped her mouth with a paper napkin.

For some reason, Christopher knew he could trust me, perhaps because I was the only adult who wouldn't try to reform him. I thought of him as more of an artist than an arsonist and more of a gardener, really, than a fire starter. The fire was his creation, each one a unique event, each burning a little different from the last depending on how and where he had chosen to grow the flames. Oxygen, fuel, and heat were his fertilizer, rain, and sunlight. His gardens bloomed in the instant it took for the sparks he scattered like seeds to take root in junkyards, empty houses, and old buildings.

"Why?" I had asked him, brushing a biscuit crumb off my faded jeans.

Kristen stared out the window at the parking lot where Zach waited for me, leaning against his Mustang, the top down as he lit a cigarette.

"I don't want to let them die," Christopher said, his hand on the ashtray I had been using while smoking the few cigarettes I had borrowed from Mother's purse. "I'm the one who made them, and they're mine. I have to save them. No one else will."

He was glaring at my silver lighter. Sighing, I picked up the lighter and put it in my pocket before taking a long drag and crushing my cigarette against the glass. He seemed disappointed, so I let my lighter fall from my pocket as I got up from the table. Without a word, he scooted the lighter slyly, holding it between his shoes. While I took the bills from my wallet, he bent down as if to tie his shoes, but his shoes were already tied.

As I took a last swig of bitter coffee, Libby nodded to me and a chill ran down my back. I realized I might have known her son better than she ever would. He was a creator like I was. He made bad things happen, but they were his disasters and he loved them in a different way than he loved the disasters that were not his own.

I left a big tip on the table for his mother that day. Christopher hugged her hard before walking out the back door. Kristen followed him.

Outside the diner, Zach opened the passenger-side door of his Mustang for me, and I climbed in, looking back at Christopher and Kristen as they walked toward the cinema, which was only a short distance from the diner, just two blocks away. He held her hand and flicked my lighter every time she turned away to look at the Mustang. Zach and I waved as we passed them by.

Outside of the burning cinema, lights flashed and sirens blared while Libby got into the ambulance behind Christopher. She went with him without a word, and I felt more worried for her than I did for the boy. Somehow I knew he would be all right, but I wasn't so certain about her.

Maybe because Kristen needed something to hold onto after Christopher had been taken away, she caught a large piece of ash drifting like an autumn leaf through the sultry air and crushed the ash in her hand before licking up the gray powder. The children followed her example, making strange faces as they licked the ash from their palms.

That day I was surprised by what the children did because I was no longer a child and my teenage years were spent forgetting the things children do. But now that I have children of my own, I'm not surprised by anything. Children will put anything except for food in their mouths as long as they see someone else taste it first. Foil or paper would have worked for the children just as well as ashes, but ashes were what we had that day.

The children seemed to grow hungrier by the minute and kept catching the ash like precious manna and licking each other's palms as if the ash were nourishing and somewhat delicious, a miracle and a delicacy that took on an acquired taste.

"No," Kristen said, even though she was still picking her teeth.

Ash caught on the cottonwood seeds, and the sight of the seeds drifting made me short of breath.

"You'll make yourselves sick," I scolded the children.

"Why?" Tina Borne asked, dropping her doll on the pavement.

"Because you're eating that awful stuff."

"How come?"

"I don't know."

"Why?" she asked again.

"How about this," I said, my heart beating fast, "I'll ask you why in about ten or fifteen years and if you still remember then you can tell me."

"Why?"

"Because you'll be a big girl then."

"How come?"

Because you're going to eat and eat and just keep eating like everyone else in your goddamned family and you won't know how to stop and you'll get big and fat like your mother and her sisters. But I didn't say anything to her. I knew when I was beaten. Since there was no kind way to answer her, I just picked up her doll and handed it to her before walking away.

I realized that perhaps it was a good thing that the children were devouring the ashes of the old cinema because it was burning to the ground and would probably never be rebuilt. The smoky taste alone would make them remember what was lost, even when they were elderly and I was dead or going by another name in another place and the rest of the town had forgotten the cinema. As Kristen crushed more ash to gray powder, I wondered what it tasted like to her and the children. To me, the powder tasted like Zach Corson's old cigarettes littering the floor of his Mustang, but I didn't want to think of Zach at a time like that. He had refinished his car and painted it a startling green, the color of the oak leaves at dawn.

"For some reason," he had once told me in the evening while he was playing with Kristen's hair, "this color of green makes me think of you."

It was my eyes, I realized, but never told him.

"Not now," I whispered so softly I thought no one else could hear. "Don't think of his hands."

Kristen looked at me.

It was too late. I could hear him saying her name, could feel his voice vibrating against my ear, and could feel the tug of his lips catching on strands of her long hair, even though he was nowhere in sight. In moments like these, pulling nervously on her shell barrettes, I hated myself, and yet I realized how lucky she was.

No one knew what to make of us because I was better at keeping her secrets than I was at keeping my own. I was no angel on those nights I tried to kiss her full on the mouth right after kissing him. She didn't like my mouth open on hers, so I slipped my tongue into her ear, and she slapped me while Zach laughed. On those nights, he parked his Mustang beside deserted country roads, the radio blaring southern rock as the headlights went dark. The tires rolled softly through the leaves before stopping in the moonlit field.

While I sat in the front seat, watching them, I started a hundred fires that never burned anywhere except in my heart. There were ashes all around me long before Christopher's fires destroyed buildings all over town. I set myself apart from others, who would judge me or forgive me or envy me, depending on who they were and who they assumed I was. Even before I dyed my hair candy-apple red and learned to speak the lost language of silence, I assumed that nothing I did would ever really matter, but Christopher proved me wrong.

As I walked away from Zach and Kristen, alone in the darkness as I would one day walk away from that town and toward another, it seemed to me that my mistakes were what made their luck. He loved her more each night because of what I did, and I knew I would love him for the rest of my days even though he would forget my name the moment I was gone.

CHAINS

In the woods near the picnic tables, years ago, when Meg was a child, she heard teenagers whispering to each other about her father's crying. On the fountain walls, the white paint faded away under crosses and encrypted symbols of gangs long gone and hearts with girls' names spray-painted inside. Her father painted circus animals on the fountain—elephants and tigers and lions and hippos. His sprawling circus dominated the graffiti with white roses of cotton candy clouds in the sky above royal blue tents, cadmium-red hoops of fire, and huge muscular beasts with bright, intelligent eyes. Often he cried when his animals were painted over by the graffiti artists in the park. Sometimes when one of his favorite animals was defaced, he disappeared for weeks so that Meg wondered if he was ever coming back.

Her childhood was marred by his leaving, just as his painted animals were marred by teenagers who laughed as he cried, smearing the tigers with silver chains.

Ashes clung to curtains inside the log cabin where her mother played harmonica, the songs her father loved, songs about the railroad and men who worked nights returning to sleeping children. Her mother's metallic music drifted through open windows like rain, the melody inviting him to come back home.

Remnants of Meg's childhood littered the living room, a stuffed monkey made of yarn, a large ventriloquist's dummy dressed like Donald Duck, and a naked Rainbow Bright doll turned upside down on the windowsill. She once loved that doll more than anything in the world, and it bothered her to see the doll abandoned. But because her father's circus had been painted over again, or because she was pregnant and hadn't yet told her mother, she was too embarrassed to pick the doll up and dress it and put it in the rocking chair where it used to sit.

As she lit a cigarette, a man's hand reached through the open window to graze the doll's foot. The hand lifted the doll into the air by its bright red hair, and the doll was gone.

She opened the door and saw her father stroking the doll's hair, dirty fingers catching on tangled yarn. With his new beard, he looked like a much older man. He was dangling a handful of silver jewelry, which he held out to Meg. She didn't want to put the necklaces on, but she put them on anyway. Tangling and untangling, the tingling silver dazzled her in moonlight.

As her mother approached her father, fingers running through his matted beard, he ignored her and only looked toward Meg. The necklaces left dark marks on her hands when she touched them and made her neck itch. She was afraid to ask where the necklaces had come from.

"You're pregnant?" he whispered.

She didn't answer.

After entering the house, he kept dropping his cigarette in the wrong places, forgetting to snuff out the tip. He set the couch on fire, and Meg's mother killed the flames with the fire extinguisher that flooded the room with white powder. Meg could barely see her parents' faces through smoke-haze. They were coughing, and she could hardly breathe. But the fire was out. Her mother opened a window as her father clutched the doll to his chest.

"Hank," her mother yelled, "for God's sake."

"What have you done?" Meg asked.

"Hell," he said.

"You drink too much," her mother said to her father, "and you smell bad."

"I smell?" he asked, sniffing the doll.

Meg wanted a cup of coffee and offered him one. He refused and she suspected he had never liked her coffee because she mixed Maxwell House with Folgers Crystals.

Before he left that night, he asked to take the doll with him. She was drinking coffee with her mother. They held the warm cups in their hands, waving to him on the dark porch as he drove away singing a lullaby, buckling the doll into the passenger's seat as if it were a child riding beside him.

"Say bye-bye, Rainbow Bright," her mother whispered as if to the wind. "Say bye-bye, Daddy."

Meg didn't want to say anything, so she went inside to pour herself another cup of the bittersweet coffee that tasted of metal, ashes, oatmeal, stale cigarettes, roses, rancid cashews, and candles.

A month later, Meg noticed her belly's reflection in the lake. As she stood on the shore, her mother and father whispered to each other about the chains. The girl's body drifted slowly, and the boat stalled. When the boat reached the shore, men were tugging the chains, taking up the slack, dragging the body to the grasses.

The girl's hair was full of mud, and some of the mud was coming off on the rocks. The sheriff put a towel over the girl's face, or rather the place where her face used to be. People crowded closer to look at the body before the coroner came to take it away. The girl's skin was gray. Her chest was torn, and her broken ribs resembled driftwood.

Meg's father stared at the lake and hid the doll inside the folds of his army jacket, hunched against what he concealed as he crept along the muddy shore.

Meg followed the sound of laughter in the trees and found her father dancing in the moonlit park. The darkness of oak shadow surrounded him as he spun the doll above his head. Cigarette butts floated in rainwater under the golden monkeys he had painted. The monkeys' red hats burned above slender necks encircled in delicate chain. The chain stretched outside the frame of concrete wall behind the fountain, tethers unseen.

The shadow of the doll's hair hid his gaze in darkness.

Meg watched in silence. The way he caressed the doll with tenderness and pure, undisguised joy—wonder, even—made Meg shiver. She couldn't bring herself to turn away. The doll was filthy, stained, torn. It hurt her that her father seemed to love the doll more in spite of its stains.

She took a step closer to him. He stopped twirling.

"Who are you?" he asked, approaching.

"You're my father," she whispered, unwilling to look at his eyes. Not wanting to see his face, his expression, she focused on his old boots, the thick, uneven crust of caked filth that clung to the snakeskin.

"I know who I am," he said, spitting on the grass. "Who the hell are you?"

"Meg."

She looked at his eyes, his wide clear eyes, and saw his face was splotched, splattered with what appeared to be black paint, almost dry. His hands were glistening with the dark substance that stained the doll.

"Meg?" he whispered.

He stepped closer and held the doll out to her. She knew better than to back away.

She pretended to admire the doll.

"She's dirty, ain't she?" he asked, his lip trembling.

That's when Meg smelled blood. He stepped into a patch of moonlight and the redness glistened—blood drying on the doll, his face, his hands, his boots.

"Ain't she?" he asked, again.

"Let's give her a bath," Meg said, leading him to the fountain.

They knelt beside the fountain, dunking the doll into the murky water. Ripples of blood ebbed as she reached down to touch his fingers, rubbing her hands against his, holding his wrists.

Once the blood washed away from his skin, Meg was sorry to see that he had no wounds, that the blood was not his own.

"Our baby," he whispered, gesturing with his bearded chin toward the wet doll, limp and heavy in his hands.

Meg almost took the doll from him, then reminded herself that it was just an old toy. She imagined her baby forming like a secret inside and tried to think of ways to keep it away from him.

"Who died?" she asked, speaking to him as if he were a naughty child. "Whose blood is this?"

He laughed at her.

When he was asleep in his car, she pried the doll from his hands.

———

The police, displeased with her for washing the doll, wanted certain incriminating details, and she knew what she looked like during the interviews—the unfortunate pregnant girl talking to the young detective.

"The doll," he said, "could prove useful, whether or not a victim is located."

Thinking of the body in the lake, she studied the doll on the desk and wondered what her father would do once he realized the doll was gone. Wrapped in thick, clear plastic, the doll looked like trash, like cloth and yarn and plastic that had been tossed away with scraps from the butcher's shop.

"He's a good man," she whispered.

The detective left the room and rushed back, his short hair wet with perspiration.

"We found him in his car and the lady in the trees behind the fountain."

"How is he?"

"She's dead, and your mother wants to take you home. I don't want you to go with her. Okay?"

"Why?"

"He's asking for you. He says he wants the doll back, says he needs it. Says he will only talk to you. Get him to write it down. It will be easier that way."

———

When her father looked at her, he began to whimper.

"I want to make things right," he whispered.

"Write it in a letter to me," Meg said.

He reached for the pen, pulled the paper closer and hunched over the pages for hours—sighing, snorting, growling, and ripping at the tablet before he was finished.

Afterward, he handed the pages to Meg and slept for hours. He would never talk about what he had written.

"It's not much, but it's enough," the detective said, relieved.

The letter, which looked as short and sloppy as she expected, was much more coherent than she imagined, although as a confession it never made much sense. Her father's tears had turned the paper soggy and fragile so that the pages dried crisp and brittle, wrinkled. His words read as follows:

> Darling, I saw her in the parking lot, one of the people from old times. But she wasn't old. She was as young as she ever was. She saw me. She knew. I walked to her. She walked to me. I touched her. Hi, ya, she said, as always she said to me when I was a boy. You remember me? Yes. You remember what happened? Yes. Can you do it just like you saw it? Yes. You will? Yes. You remember what it

*looked like? Oh, yes. Pretend like I am it and you are the
one with the chains. The chains are in the trees. You'll find
them there. Pretend like I am not me. Do it, just like you
saw it. Don't stop, no matter what, until it's finished—
even if I tell you to stop, even if I beg. Understand? Yes, I
said. Then, I did.*

After Meg's baby was born, her father kept asking the police if he could have the doll back, but the doll wasn't really
a doll anymore, just hunks of molded cloth, wispy stuffing,
mashed plastic, and frayed yarn. Somehow he just couldn't
understand. He still wanted the old doll, now more than ever,
and even began to write Meg letters about the doll although
she claimed she had no idea what had become of it.

"Where is she?" He kept asking. "What happened? I
don't remember what happened. Where did she go? Please,
I just want to hold her and hold her."

Meg visited him in prison with her son in her arms, the
boy burping milk on her shoulders as he smiled at her father.
She wanted to tell her father what her life was like now that
she had a child, but sometimes she found it hard to explain
things to him. He had no patience for her stories about raising the child. In fact, he didn't want to talk about his grandson, the boy she had named after him. He only wanted to
talk about the baby elephant from his childhood that was
beaten to death after refusing to perform a circus act.

"He was screaming and trying to crawl away on his
knees like a human being," her father said.

Putting her hands over her son's ears and smiling at
her father as if nothing were wrong, the way she sometimes

smiled when he was near, she imagined her father as a boy watching the elephant die, but she couldn't imagine the expression on his face. Secretly, she suspected that if the elephant had died another way her father would have been another type of man. He might have been free, holding his grandson in the open air and laughing at the park, carrying the child near the fountain.

A week before her father was sentenced to die, someone sent her a weapon that looked like a small flashlight. The package had no return address. The note, which wasn't signed, read:

> *This will render any attacker helpless and is safe to use on animals and persons under the influence of alcohol and narcotics.*

After unwrapping the weapon from its clear package, she turned off all the lights in her house. Her son cried for joy as she flipped on the switch and pointed the weapon at the windows, but it was only a tiny light shining in the dark.

ETCHER

Drew heard Wendy's breath spill out of her mouth, the delicate sound of glass falling through air. He would have stepped in to save almost any other girl. But Wendy was different. She was a smoker, so she didn't flinch when she was close to fire.

Sampler took a little bottle of purple fluid out of his coat pocket and began to pour the fluid over her jeans. "Want me to light it?" he asked Wendy, who was twisting a long blue ribbon into her braid while holding a lit cigarette expertly in her teeth.

"Loser," she said, "go on."

"Want me to set your jeans on fire?" Sampler asked.

"Do it!" said Drew.

Sampler poured more fluid onto her jeans and set them on fire. Wendy screamed as the long flame flared. But the fire died quickly as the fluid ran out, and her jeans didn't burn. There were no ashes, holes, or evidence that the fire had ever been lit, yet she was crazed with anger, taking a big bite out of her cigarette and chewing as if it were food.

Drew spat on the ground near Sampler's shoes. Even outside of Mr. Loamer's class, Sampler used chemistry to trick people's eyes. Sampler was a waste of everybody's time,

Drew thought: hell to look at, slouching shoulders and a crummy black hat made of felt-covered cardboard. His voice screeching like crickets, all Sampler ever talked about was his experiments. He was a scrawny kid, always twirling the long chain dangling off his belt loop.

"Don't you get it?" Sampler asked Wendy, laughing. "I bet you were scared. I bet you thought I was going to burn your legs, hey Wendy?"

"I wish you had," she said, putting her finger over the dark spot behind her chipped tooth.

Sampler let go of the little bottle. It shattered at Drew's feet.

"Watch the shoes," Drew said.

Even though it was the middle of August, Sampler wore a trench coat full of tiny moth-holes. As he tried to scurry away, the coat blew open behind him, the slit in the back separating into two dusty wings. Hoping that Wendy was watching, Drew pretended to strike Sampler across the forehead. Sampler's black hat flew off, and he moaned, reaching out as it was swept away. Close up, his spiked hair skittered over his forehead. Drew imagined punching Sampler's face, but shuddered at the thought of chattering teeth, gashes, and shut eyes.

———

At home, Drew saw a black and yellow spider bouncing on its web outside his front door. He thought about stomping it, but he had never seen one that size or that color. He decided to leave it for a while.

When his hands came closer to the web, the spider bounced faster. He figured he had enough trouble that day, so he reached out to tear the spider down.

He jumped back, startled by his sister's eyes on the other side of the window. He realized now Carlie had been watching all this time. Almost twenty years old, she was too old to be living in their parents' house, but their mother had let her turn the upstairs room into a studio. Carlie spent her days sculpting figures that weren't really human but old children that crawled out of fountains, wings sharper than teeth, eyes as vacant as the darkness behind their gaping mouths.

Drew opened the front door, careful not to dislodge the spider testing its web. He wanted to say something nice to Carlie, but the longer he looked at her the more he wondered what the hell had gone wrong. Wendy, he thought, had changed Carlie for the worst. He rarely saw Carlie except when she was whispering to Wendy across her tiny studio with wind through the open window blowing the dry pulp of shredded newspaper into their hair.

Carlie's hands started shaking whenever she had trouble finding buyers for her sculptures. She ate less, grew thin, and worked harder than ever. The palms of her hands were always inky with newsprint. As she shredded the papers, she occasionally tucked a scrap into the back of her cheek, let it grow soft and gummy in there.

Still chewing the paper, she pointed to the spider, calming down now that Drew was on the other side of the window. "You like it," she said. "I saw you."

"Hell, no."

"I watched what you were doing. You were about to stroke it."

———

That evening Drew saw Sampler standing outside the front door, examining the spider with a magnifying glass. Clinching his fists, he wanted to teach Sampler a lesson, but first he had to get Carlie away from the window. She was tapping on the glass, trying to get the spider to move.

"Who is that boy out there?" she asked.

"Just a jerk I've got to take care of."

"One of your friends from school?"

"He's not a friend," said Drew.

"You know what it is?" Sampler asked, his voice muffled behind the windowpane.

"Yeah."

"A banana spider. Can I have it?"

"No," Carlie said, "it's mine."

Before she could open the door, Drew hammered the glass with his fists.

Sampler ran away, laughing.

———

Since his project was due the next day, Drew decided he had better start working. The experiment he chose was the simplest one, a miniature volcano hollowed out and filled with vinegar and baking soda to mimic an eruption. He figured he could just sit back, counting on Carlie to make the volcano.

"I need your help," Drew said.

Carlie started squeezing her hands together like she had just burnt her fingers and wanted to cover them up so no one would know how badly she was hurt. He thought how easy it would be to pull her hands apart to see if she was hiding something. Instead, he told her about the project, and she began to talk in an excited tone, looking out the window as if she could already see the volcano looming.

"I'll do it in a second," she said, "but promise me something first."

Drew thought about plucking the clots of newspaper out of her tangled hair. He wanted to help her in some way but didn't know how. He put one hand over her mouth to quiet her. "I know someone's up there," he said, taking the hand down and wiping his palm on his jeans. "I won't tell."

Wendy was smoking a twisted cigarette in his sister's studio, her huge eyes doctored in bright makeup, the brown mascara caked up like dusty fiddlebacks dancing on her lashes. He hated seeing Wendy in Carlie's room. Wendy belonged at school, he thought, not in the house he came home to. The longer she stayed in his house, the more she reminded him of his problems.

It seemed to Drew that everything Wendy collected accumulated in the upstairs: tattered jeans, spaghetti jars full of cigarettes, glittering shards of ruined jewelry.

She was the perfect artist's model and a great help to his sister in her work. Wendy could hold a position for hours, barely blinking her eyes. She made a game of trying to scare Drew, but he wasn't playing. Whenever she was posing for Carlie, Drew tried to talk to her, but she wouldn't respond, wouldn't blink, wouldn't breathe. He hated the way she could just sit there staring, asleep with her eyes open. He thought she was laughing behind her calm face. When she looked up at him like that, her gaze imperceptibly shifting as he moved, he had to smile, realizing how easily he could shake her awake.

Some of the sculptures of her were as small as dolls. Some were larger than women. The large ones scared Drew's mother. She wouldn't go into Carlie's studio anymore. The room had gone claustrophobic with the shape of Wendy's body from all angles stretching out in perfect proportion. The walls were a dusty white. The painted sculptures loomed red and gold. Shadows cascaded dull over every solid form. The narrow shapes of women, long and hideous, stretched over the walls and ceiling, the brittle fabric of their dresses leaping like flames, bracelets of chain dangling off their naked arms. Even the sleepers reached for each other, their hands open on the air. Their hair was treated grass Carlie had uprooted from neglected fields. Their teeth, the ivory chipped off old piano keys.

At traveling arts festivals, Carlie had tried to sell her sculptures only to find out she couldn't give them away. She claimed people spent their money on photos of children blooming from giant flowers. Buyers weren't interested in taking home life-size figures celebrating human suffering and the postures of impending doom.

Drew noticed the longer Carlie sculpted, the more she shaped faces like Wendy's and her own: wild, thick-lashed eyes hollowed out by hunger, filth, and shadow. She often forgot to eat, sculpting emaciated figures crouching low or opening their thin skin like long coats to show the brittle bones and shriveled organs the flesh could not hide.

Inside the sunlit studio, Wendy sat on the bare floor tearing newspapers into long strips. She stopped for a moment to move the paper away from Drew. As she stood up, he heard the wooden panels give, then realized it was the creaking of her bones. She stretched her arms, her fingers rustling a sculpture's dusty hair.

Carlie smiled at Wendy then got right to work, slapping some pulp of glue and shredded paper down onto a wooden base. She worked her hands in a succession of frenzied blows. Her palms pounded the soft mixture into a solid, mounded form. Her dainty fingers probed the volcano's surface for imperfections.

"I need a hole for the vinegar," he said.

"Is this big enough?" Carlie asked, scraping out a place in the center with her filthy fingernails.

"What is this?" He pointed to a figure of a child wearing a black, paper hat.

"Now we've just got to let it dry." She stood back to survey her work.

"Looks great," Drew said, making his way past the sculptures. On his way out, he reached for the black hat resting precariously on the sculpture's tilted head.

"Not so fast," Carlie said, taking the hat away from him. "Now we've got to paint it."

"No. This is good enough."

"We could gather some sticks, leaves, and grass to make a village scene," Carlie said, touching the wooden base.

"What about your project?" Drew asked Wendy.

"What makes you think I'm doing one?" she asked, the cigarette bobbing from the hole in her tooth.

"Go ahead and fail the class. You think I care?"

Even though it was dark outside, Wendy climbed out onto the balcony and down a white ladder into the backyard. The rails crackled under her slight weight like paper on fire. The ladder held, the wood splintering. The wind picked up, cluttering Wendy's hair. Drew wondered how long it would take for her to reach the ground. On her way back up, she climbed slowly. The twigs were tucked into her shirt.

Carlie slumped over the little village, her hands arranging pine needles, sticks, and wild flowers on the wooden stand. Her sculptures' perfect forms towered over her scrawny, hunched body. Seeing her like that made Drew think something terrible was going to happen to her.

In the corner, Wendy fell asleep, coiled into a tight ball, her arms hugging her knees. Drew pretended to give her a single kick, just to see if she would move.

———

That night Carlie took a lamp from her studio and shone the light on the spider crouching outside the downstairs window. She tried to attract moths, the light luring insects into the sprawling web. The glare made the shadow bounce in frenzied motions.

A fat, dusty moth tangled its wings in the gauzy light. The spider pounced low. The wings flailed for just an instant before the spider's legs, like agile fingers, twirled the moth into a tightly spun sack dangling on the web.

Until then, Drew never knew how pretty it was to watch something die. Another moth touched down, this one as green as a new leaf. The spider didn't bother to wrap it up but held the second moth down, clutching the whole nervous body as it relaxed in the lamplight. The bright green of the wings faded into the dullest gray he could remember.

Outside the window, Drew saw a figure in a long coat ride by on a bicycle. He cursed, imagining Sampler capturing the spider in a jar and studying it under the glass. But the spider was still safe in its web.

Drew heard the balcony wood shifting, Wendy in the rocking chair lulling the night away. A single cricket leapt, then landed near Carlie, rubbing its legs together. Drew stomped it with his bare foot, smearing it into the tile. His parents were getting ready for bed, but Carlie was still mesmerized by the spider jumping in the light she shone through the window.

In the morning, Drew's mother drove him to school early so he could take his project to science class before first bell. He held the huge, sculpted volcano dwarfing the tiny village on the wooden plank.

Standing outside the building, he pounded on the glass of the locked doors. Teachers walked by on the inside. Mrs. Raleigh opened the door.

"What is it?" she asked.

"I need to take my project in," he said, feeling himself towering over her.

"Well, Mr. Loamer hasn't informed me of this."

"Can I just come in?" he asked.

"I could get in trouble for this," she said, her small body blocking the way.

He thought how easy it would be to shove her aside. "Look," he said, "I've got this big thing to carry. I'm not doing this for my health."

"I don't have the authorization," she said as she closed the door on his shoe.

From behind the glass, he watched her walk away. Then Wendy Walker slipped out from the other side of the vending machines and ran to open the door.

"Carlie does nice work," she said.

Her hair was a jumbled mess of curly and straight, a bunch of lousy colors mixed together. She held a pencil in her mouth. Reaching into her hip pocket, she pulled out a small, painted leaf. She handed it to Drew, but he didn't want to take it. He nodded down at the volcano in his hands. She put the gold leaf into the center hole where all the vinegar was going to be.

"Give that to Carlie," Wendy said. "Tell her I found it."

As she slipped away down the hall, he saw her bending over, picking up little scraps of colored paper. She found trash on the ground, broken sticks, torn flowers, green glass, tiny, glinting pieces of copper. All of this, he imagined, she would offer Carlie. He planned to crush it into a powder before tossing it out the window of Carlie's studio when no one else was looking.

———

Drew carried the volcano into the classroom where Wendy was pretending to smoke her gnawed-off pencil like she would a long cigarette. He put the volcano down on the project table: fish tanks full of marbles and colored water, tiny plants bright green and just beginning to sprout inside egg cartons, a toy car made of four records, a mouse trap on wheels, and some string.

"Know what I think?" she asked, the pencil clacking against her chipped teeth.

"No."

"Not too many people understand smoking the way I do."

"You should know."

"I'm serious. Five or six minutes and then it's gone. You watch it disappear. You see in the ashes the disappearance of time, and it has nothing to do with days or hours. It's just the minutes, the seconds, you know?" The tardy bell rang, and she jumped like the kids who ran into the classroom were running after her. The pencil snapped on her broken teeth. "Damn," she said, "I really need a cigarette."

———

By the time Mr. Loamer walked into the classroom, Wendy was making a bracelet out of locks of her hair knotted with colored string. Her ring-jeweled fingers reflected the window light more flinty and mysterious than the green glass she had slipped into her pocket.

Loamer began lecturing on chapter nine. Drew reached into his backpack and noticed his book wasn't there. He raised his hand.

"What is it?" Loamer asked, pointing his good ear in Drew's direction.

Mr. Loamer was completely deaf in one ear and hard of hearing in the other. When Loamer wasn't looking, Drew and the rest of the football team pounded their fists into the plaster. With one kick, their big shoes went right through. Repairmen had to keep coming to fix holes in the classroom walls.

Drew screamed until he felt the veins popping out on his neck, "Someone stole my book."

"Again?"

"Yeah."

"Well," Loamer said, putting his hands on the back of his head, "I was afraid that was what you were saying. Come here, boy." He started to whisper. "I didn't want to embarrass anyone, but I heard what you were saying all along. Why don't you go and ask that girl over there?" He motioned to Wendy Walker with one nod of his bald head, the bones of his skull making the bare skin shine as they surfaced, the white light pooling over his cranium.

Wendy flipped through the pages as if she had never seen the pictures before, men riding bicycles, vials of purple fluid, airplanes taking off over water, helium balloons lost in the clouds, a cartoon of a human body with all the skin peeled off.

"Whose book is that?" Drew asked her. He reached out and grabbed one of the corners.

"I was just reading it," she said, pulling the book away.

"Don't you have a book of your own?"

"Lost it. Can we share?"

He put his hands on the cover. "I want my chemistry book back."

"I'm going to tell," Wendy said. She grabbed the book and stumbled to Loamer's desk where she started crying. Loamer called to Drew after Wendy ran out into the hallway.

"Why did you do it?" Loamer whispered.

"I didn't do anything," Drew said.

"She claims you threatened to kill her if she didn't hand it over. You could be suspended or expelled for this, or worse, Etcher. Much, much worse."

"I'll take care of it," Drew said.

"How?"

While Mr. Loamer was turned away, Drew slipped past the project table. He wanted to find Wendy and bring her back to class before he presented his volcano. She was hiding behind the school building and smoking a real cigarette.

"You can have the book if you want it," Drew said, thinking how sharp a chipped tooth could be and how easy it would be to close her open smile.

She put out the cigarette and leaned against the brick wall, absently weaving hair and string.

"What's the deal with my sister, anyhow?" Drew asked.

"Wouldn't you like to know," Wendy said, handing him the tightly knotted bracelet too small for his wrist.

Soon after Drew and Wendy went back to class, Allen Sampler walked in, his trench coat a dirty mess of tangled strings. For the first time since Drew had known him, Sampler's shoulders weren't slouching over. Even while setting the huge wooden box on the project table, Sampler kept himself in good posture.

"Ready for me?" Sampler asked, a terrible smell filling the room as he twirled his silver chain.

He took the lid off the box. Inside was the duck experiment, twenty dead baby ducks at different stages of hatching. He had killed them by sticking straight pins into their skulls, the black and yellow down brittle with dry yolk.

"Well," Mr. Loamer said, "twenty million babies are killed every year by their own mothers."

"This experiment demonstrates the various stages of infantile development," Sampler said, starting in on his project speech. "You'll see here the dissected egg just before hatching."

Shifting in his chair, Drew leaned away from the black, wooden box. "Why did you do it, Sampler?"

"They didn't do anything to you," Wendy said.

"You little shit," Drew said.

"Now if everyone will please just calm down," Sampler said, staring at the box as if the ducks were about to hatch. "I'll be happy to answer any questions to put your minds at ease."

"Did it hurt?" Wendy asked, raising her left hand from the front row. She covered her nose with her right.

"No. I poked the needle through to the brain. But most weren't even at that stage where they could feel pain yet. See this one is still an embryo," he said, pointing to a speck of dried blood.

"You cruel, worthless bastard!" Drew kept shouting.

"Everybody, please. Just listen." Sampler wiped his hands on his trench coat. "All I ask is ten minutes of your time, ten minutes like everybody else got."

"Why don't you pick on somebody your own size?"

"Just five minutes. Just two." A cigarette slipped through a hole in Sampler's coat pocket. Watching it fall, he touched the tips of his spiked hair as if he had forgotten the black hat was no longer there. "This took me a long time, a whole month in the garage. I had to find good eggs. I had to rent an incubator."

"I hope somebody sticks a pin through your skull, Sampler."

Sampler reached for the hat, letting one hand linger over his forehead. "You're not likely to see something like this again," he said, straightening his collar. "We all know you've never seen it before."

"No one should have to see this shit," said Drew.

"You don't understand. I stopped them at just the right stages. I had to keep a journal," he said, taking out a rumpled lab manual from his coat flap.

"Thank you, Allen," Mr. Loamer said, putting the lid on the box. "You can sit down now."

Sampler kept touching his head as if he hadn't been there to watch the hat blow away. Even when Drew went up to present his project, the gold leaf on the inside bubbling over, Sampler was still standing there looking at the box.

In the halls by the lockers, Sampler got away, but Drew held on to the trench coat. The material was so brittle with filth that it fell apart like old paper. Drew stayed long enough to watch Sampler come crouching back, the chain gliding through his fingers as he let go to pick up the disintegrating heap. Sampler threw the trench coat back over his shoulders even though by now it wasn't really a coat anymore.

After examining the torn coat, Mr. Loamer gave Drew a choice of twenty days of two-hour detentions or the task of planting trees in front of the school. What Loamer didn't tell him was that each tree weighed over seventy pounds and was supposed to take two people to lift. It took Drew only thirty minutes to plant eight trees.

When Carlie and Wendy pulled the convertible up to the school lawn and started honking, the trees were swooping, leaning against each other in precarious tepees. The afternoon sunlight through the leaves cast odd shadows on the center. The wind moved the leaves. The yard was full of loose dirt and chunks of dislodged grass broken on the sidewalk.

Carlie kept honking so Drew had to get into the car. He felt his friends watching him as Carlie drove off. The car was full of newspapers he and Wendy had to lie on just to keep the papers from flying away.

―――――

The next morning before the first bell rang, the whole school was gathered in the front yard. The trees were wobbling, still leaning on each other. They would have to be replanted before the limbs began to snap off. Mr. Loamer paced the yard with both of his hands clutching his bald head.

Wendy crawled out from inside one of the tepees just before the trees collapsed. She looked up at Drew as she stood, holding a long strand of tangled ribbon. As she moved closer to him, he tried to look at anyone but her. Sampler was examining the leaves of a fallen tree. Wendy was holding the ribbon high over her hair. Drew didn't want her to give it to him, not when everybody else was watching to see what he would do.

"Let me come over to your house after school," Sampler said, smiling.

"What for?" asked Drew.

Wendy was looking right at him, her lips barely moving.

"I've got something important to tell your sister about her spider," Sampler said.

"You stay away from her."

"Don't say I didn't warn you." Sampler said, scratching a place behind his ear.

That night the lamp began to shake in Carlie's hands, causing the light to ricochet off the inside walls. Drew couldn't stand the circle of light leaping off the house like it was following a spider on the inside, so he took Carlie's hands into his own. He steadied her just enough so together they could shine the lamp outside the window.

She was scrawny but pretty in her own way, he thought. She just didn't like to leave her sculptures, her spider, Wendy, or whatever project she was working on. He heard the distant rumble of the highway behind the house and for an instant felt a little glimmer of hope flare like a winged insect picking up the headlights before splattering on a windshield.

"I want to hold her," she said, tapping on the glass. "Could you get her down for me?"

"Why do I have to be the one to do it?"

"You're the only one who's not afraid to touch her."

He went out the front door, leaving Carlie on the inside. The spider bounced on its web every time he reached out. He knew it wouldn't be easy to preserve the way Carlie wanted. The spider had already lost one long, yellow leg trying to get away but began first to creep and then to crawl into his open hand. She was smaller than she looked up in the web. In the high corner, one perfectly spherical, cream-colored ball of eggs dangled. The bright spots on her began to fade away until she was as gray as the moths she had sucked dry. He reached out to tear down the eggs, but then thought better of it. His sister was still shining the light in the window, trying to get the moths to fly into the dusty web even though the eggs had already been laid and she had to know the spider was going to die anyway.

Inside the house, he opened his cupped hands.

"Is that all she was?" Carlie asked.

As Carlie stroked the spider's legs with her delicate fingers, he wanted to get away from her. He couldn't stand the way she kept looking at the wilted spider in his hands, so he brushed the crumpled body into her inky palm and left her beside the window.

Climbing the stairs, he imagined the shadow of the leaves in the wind skittering over the moonlight on Wendy's scrawny arms. He heard the wood on the studio balcony let out a long, creaking sigh. Outside the glass door, an empty chair rocked in the wind. Wendy was walking the balcony rail, her hair blowing into a tangled frenzy, the tips of her fingers just touching the trees. He was going to tell her to be careful but thought better of it. Even calling her name could startle her and make her fall. He was tired of watching her, tired of standing in silence in the dark room.

When he turned on the lamp, he saw only the huge reflection of himself in the glass. He was standing over his sister's sculptures as the shadows fell from ceiling to floor. Smelling the dry grass, tapping the chipped piano keys, he thought about how brittle their newspaper bodies were. Even the wind could harm them. Suddenly, he felt powerful and alone. He never knew he could be both thrilled and sorry that everyone around him was fragile. Gently, he reached out to touch the wrist of one of the sculptures. Except for her long blue legs and green hair made of wispy synthetic feathers, she was like all the others. He could break any one of them into little bits, and no one could do anything about it.

VISION OF MIRRORS

As a young man, Father spent hours in front of mirrors, a hopeful actor training his eyes to express loneliness. On cue, under stage lights, a cadmium hemorrhage swelled over his muscled chest where the villain's knife struck, again and again. As a child, I saw him murdered on stage, and learned to await the stabbing, later dreaming the knife was in my hand.

"Why do you boys dance like women?" he asks tonight shortly after he forgets who I am. He can't recall his own name. "The bodies sparkle with translucent powder their mothers wore. They feel the need to bond to every person, telling details of their suffering. This is how men train actors in certain countries, the same way they train prostitutes."

"Really?" I whisper to the ceiling above his bed.

"I warned you," he said.

He didn't want to improve what God made gangly, the unwanted child who adored his fearful mystery. Pity passed, a hawk through night.

Every now and then, I remember the affection my father has always had for blown glass, bright and fragile and valuable, museum pieces as lovely as hollow jewels, a symbolic space I could never truly inhabit.

Details of blackouts, a dream in firelight, the shadow moving between his legs, my skeleton, as I starved, was a sign of strength smoldering inside. I needed nothing, not even food or companionship to survive. Alone, I sculpted children of paper, straw, clay, homemade glue, and disgorged newspaper. Papier-mâché became my religion, a way for me to populate a world that no one else wanted to live in. I called myself Billie because that's what my father was suddenly calling me.

"Hands trained to fend for themselves claw like dogs, stroke like fiends," he whispers.

"If you say so," I say.

"Who asked you?" he asks. "I don't know who the hell you are. Where am I?"

Love is always the far distance, the square leading out of the painting to the unseen cradle. It's true—I'm attracted to women, breasts as soft as my hands passing under thin blouses, palms cupped, fingers trembling, wrists free.

"Dance," he says, and I dance in the little hospital room until the nurses threaten to call security.

In my teenage years, gathered in darkness, I choked on thin crusts of bread. Even now, sorrow flows like wine. Men pass women drinking alcohol, washing their jeweled nipples. Stained teeth clack on bottlenecks.

Somewhere far away is a place my father once traveled where trains carry sisters between two houses, linked by a bridge. My mother was the wounded one living in a blue house with imaginary friends, weightless, dancing, feeling at home in her haven, her lovers as light as air as she wove their wings of straw. Having to be a mother to her, I became the artist she was and the child she could never be.

How many hilarious nights have I spent, weeping songs of dark-haired women into the river that ran her life? If her love were visible, she could have painted it in the years before she abandoned me, sending me back to America, to my father who could give me a better life—how terrible to know nothing lies beyond, a child who went through a world of colors.

"I'm the devil," my father whispers as he dies, "passing rain through night. I'm a sick person and all my life was sick. Your mother's blue-black hair is painted, murals over the river. Go with bridge-side guitarists, strum their women. Pass like visions, saints and whores dancing over dark water."

I'm his son and his daughter, but he doesn't know that now. I'm nowhere I want to be, just standing in this dim hospital room and wondering what he means.

Under the white paper gown, a spattering of blood shoots like red stars just as he claims he senses a child growing inside me, years before I'm reborn in the Baptist church, taking time to come back to life, hanging my head after the baptism, still wet, completely alone. He feels the jade beads of my eyes light on him, the other women in photographs frozen in time, immobilized by my youth, hands passing over a cheap blouse. On his deathbed, he's talking through metaphor—apparently, my mouth tastes of money, my face is ash and dust, my eyes are moths, the rough skin of my lipstick is red wine. My chin is lemon pulp slick with blood.

"Your mother was magnificent, not pretty," he says, his left foot twitching under thin blankets. "She was more of a man than I ever was, and that's why I wanted her. I warned her. Don't dream of marriage. There is no such thing."

"Thank you," I tell him.

"Damn straight you will," he says, as if I have just agreed to something that could make things right.

"I warned you," he said when I was just a little child, and my mother promised to become a better mother, not a better painter.

Starving herself, her head as light as water in clouds, rarely feeling the difference between night and day, she stretched canvas, elegant fingers revising thumbnail sketches. Scrawled captions begged strangers to remember her: dawn sky washed over a girl with a ribbon tied around her waist, woman in white on the blue-house patio, a trained dancer, her naked arms outstretched. Never as hungry as the mouths she wanted to feed, her hands moved over the child who gave her visions, fainting spells, violet water. Tonight fingers fly over her eyelids like fireflies above the river, and in the darkness she dreams two fireflies are my eyes so that I am with her as she finally speaks my name.

Theater of Cruelty

A balcony, a bed, a windswept curtain parting and falling, a white hand, candles reflected in distant mirrors—my actress's eyes are suddenly lit as if by fire. She stumbles across the tiered stage. Rising illumination brings her arms back into focus. Footlights peel away shadows that conceal her face and body. Motion stops. The orchestra next to the stage plays a sad melody when my actress confronts the child actor who is supposed to be a younger me. As she looks back across her shoulder, in this play, the audience never realizes that she is my sister, or rather, that she is performing the part of my deceased sister, and the child is playing the part of the boy I once was. Therefore, my actress's shoulder is my sister's shoulder, and her eyes are my sister's eyes, glazed as if awakening from a dream. Haze rises from the smog machines blasting under the floor. That haze is the fog outside the apartment windows on that evening long ago, hours before my sister was attacked and blinded in my childhood home.

She, who had raised me as if she were my mother, was raped when I was only seven years of age, shortly after I began dreaming of Shakespearean tragedies she had once read to me. The reality of what she had gone through was too painful for me to accept. Perhaps this is why I began to cultivate the notion that the world was a theater and everyone but me was merely an actor. Truly, I imagined a creative god who was putting on a performance just for me, the only real thinking being in the world. I began to believe that my sister, like the man who attacked her, was only acting.

I was living in my own Theater of Cruelty long before, as a teenager, I discovered the writings of Antonin Artaud and immediately felt a kinship with the misunderstood genius whose theories struck a chord with me because of what I had seen at a young age.

I witnessed the entire attack. Later, even though I blamed myself for not being able to save my sister, I could only identify with the attacker. Because I could not forgive myself, I forgave the evil man, and then became obsessed with reliving what I could not avenge.

The man was never found, leaving a void in my life that became the shadow side of me. Justice was never served. In order to keep my sanity, I found ways to recreate the act of violence, ways to allow me to take control over the senselessness of what changed us forever. Secretly, I've always believed this is why I became a director, why I started my own theater and became a devotee of Artaud.

———

My sister was a woman who loved to sing lullabies and to draw pictures of the characters in the lullabies. She was endlessly eating pistachios in the evenings before she sang to me. She planted red and violet tulips in the narrow garden walkways of our apartment complex.

She had such a high and clear voice, and such strong

and capable hands that could easily locate and separate bulbs clustered in the dark earth.

Long before she died, I found a way to replace her, just as I found a way to replace myself while I became the evil man in my mind. Somehow one of my sister's hands had been broken, shattered. Later, I dreamed I was the one who blinded her and I was the one who broke her hand. In dreams, I was no longer me but the man who had hurt her.

Every spring after the attack, I had to describe for her the brightness and the quality of the tulips she could no longer see. She was not the same woman, even though she had survived. She would never be the same. Neither would I. That's why the lullabies, the drawings, the tulips, and the pistachios will never appear in any of my plays.

———

Tonight, on stage, when my actress reaches her hand through the bars of the kitchen window to touch the boy's face, the boy takes hold of her hand and won't let go. He ties it into the vice; she cries out, and the audience feels her bones grinding against each other merely because of the authenticity of her screams. Some of the men in the audience rise from their seats, entranced by her performance. Just before she loses consciousness, the curtain falls, concealing her and the boy.

I run to her. When she wakes, her hand is twisted and curled like a dead spider, and she can't move her fingers, three of which are tilted backwards to her wrist.

She falls into the props, and the hollow walls slide away to reveal the rest of the cast and crew, who have to pry us apart.

"It was your finest performance," I tell her.

"Don't touch me," she says, but I hold her tightly and refuse to let go. On the way to the emergency room, she is silent in the back of the car, convulsing, collapsed against the window.

On August 21, 1963, my actress broke her hand, for the first time, on the stage above the sunset orchestra. When the scene went bad, on the blue terrace, she cried, setting the audience of travelers free to embark on more personal journeys. Through the dim streets of summer, their faces were obscured like the high leaves of distant trees nearest the black sky. I once asked her what came over her, why she did everything I told her to do, even though she must have known that it would hurt her, that it was wrong.

"It's a presence, a mood," she once said backstage in the little dressing room with the bare bulb swinging on its chain, the arc of light illuminating her pale face as she rose from her disintegrating chair. Months later, after her cast had been removed, the bones remained in a fragile arrangement and never quite healed properly as she had used the cheapest doctor she could find.

In truth, it might not have been the doctor's fault. I do not know whether or not he was a capable, competent, or trustworthy man, although I assume he wasn't yet a charlatan. Furthermore, he did warn her that certain bones never heal, not after certain types of breaks. In the years to come, beneath crates of old dresses, her disfigured hand twists and breaks again, the delicate bones hollow like a songbird's made to last through only three summers carrying the branches to nests made of simple hair and long grasses woven into song.

On sunny mornings, sparrows mate in strange patterns near my upstairs windows. Falling after rain, the wet eggs later break in the gutter, a stream of fractured limbs on the concrete ground of the theater alley. In the violet room this evening, the room with its crumbling wallpaper that leaves blue-gray dust like powder, a moonlit mist of pollen on our palms, I hear the birds calling to each other and forget where I am, why I am here—with her. Her hair is buried on the white sheets, burned into my eyes. Bruised, she is calling my name.

———

We were here, in this room. Here. Together.

Near the low cabinet stocked with red wine, the cabernet gleamed in its green bottles. I fell asleep gazing at that gleam and knowing the merlot was taken.

When I woke, my actress was snarling in her sleep beside the gray dog, Badger. Badger had been dead for twenty-seven years, his corpse perfectly preserved by a talented taxidermist who matched the dog's exact shade of blue-green eyes in glass. I hated to stare at those glass eyes. But I had to stare. They reminded me of my sister. My actress still loved Badger, the pet of her lost childhood.

"My first and only pet, the only one who will continue to love me unconditionally even after death," she said while stroking the preserved corpse.

"But what about all these cats?" I asked her.

"What about them? Cats aren't really pets because they have no souls. They're not like dogs."

"I like the cats," I said, reaching out to stroke the tabby and then the ebony tom.

"If only you were as good as Badger," she used to tell me, "if only you were as good as a dead dog, then I might love you."

I tried—oh, how I tried to be as good as Badger! I never was. No matter how I willed it to happen, I could never live up to the legacy of her dead dog.

But that was long ago. The dead dog was still alive in her for many years, along with the rest of her childhood, which is mostly gone now, even in her memory. She has no sense of self. Once the child in her had died, even Badger's ghost was lost. I felt it moving through the room, fading like smoke from an extinguished candle.

Through my actress, merlot coursed like a transfusion racing through a child's veins. As she emptied another bottle, I said, "This can't be happening, not to us."

"It happens to everyone," she whispered before tossing the bottle onto the carpet.

"The wine," I said, "the wine," and she halfway rose from the bed, looking up at me as I struck the match to light her cigarette. She refused my match and leaned into the candle flame instead, her breath raspy so that the flame danced beneath the cradle of her hair.

After taking a few drags, she gazed at me in a more personal manner, as if she suddenly recalled who I was, or rather, who I used to be. There was that hint in her eye, that strange glint. Now it seems odd to say she was afraid of me, but not as afraid as I was of myself.

"Collin," she said.

"What?" I answered back. It was the first time she had

spoken my name in over three years.

"I can't. I just can't."

The balcony doors were wide open for anyone to see what we weren't doing. The torn curtains shuttered in the night air that smelled of gasoline and steaks burning on a giant charcoal grill near the highway.

"Are you hungry?" I asked because I was. I wanted a huge steak, burnt to a crisp, even though the blackened meat sizzling on the big white plate seemed obscene. As I was still languidly contemplating the steak, she took off her gown, and wanted me to touch her. I was desperate for affection, but it had been a long time since I had sunk that low. I knew her too well, we had too much history, and the doors were still wide open.

"I'm falling," she said. "I feel myself falling when I close my eyes, then I'm spinning and falling, even though I'm still down."

I felt the need to state the obvious. "You drank too much," I said as I handed her a bunch of stale crackers to chew.

A siren wailed in the distance, and the sound grew louder before I finally saw the blue lights in the curtains, cutting into the room only to fall on the yellowed walls like ghosts in a cage.

She blew out the candles, finally, as the ambulance sped away. She closed the balcony doors, drew the curtains tight. "Dark enough for you?" she asked. I didn't answer. Why should I have? She knew my estranged and reclusive sister had been blind. She despised my dead sister more than she had ever despised any other woman and for no known reason.

I heard my actress drawing nearer, slowly, so slowly, making her way around the room as I kept moving backward to keep distance between us. When she walked to me, calling my name, her normally soft voice took on deeper tones. Playfully, she threw her voice and changed it to a husky masculine groan and then to something more feminine, higher pitched, squealing like a girl and then oinking like a pig, howling like a wolf. I wasn't amused. The whole charade was creepy, not funny, and not at all appealing.

Yet in the dark room, I was fascinated with the concept of keeping away, remaining as silent as possible as I moved while the sounds of her voice alone let me know where she was, the changing inflections the only clue to her state of mind.

Don't let her catch me, I thought. I don't know why. Suddenly, I thought of my sister, a woman without eyes. When she had regained consciousness and tried to escape that night, the man with the mask was still chasing her around the bathroom even though he had put out her eyes and was no longer wearing his mask. I felt like her, or rather the way I always assumed she must have felt later, years later, when she claimed he came back for her. When she was eighteen, that man broke into our apartment and blinded her so she couldn't see his face after he took off the mask. In the years that followed, every time I went to visit her in the hospital or the nursing home, she touched my mouth as I spoke, just to make sure I was who I said I was. I suppose it was just to make sure my voice matched my face. I was just a child when it happened, hiding in the shower behind the curtain but I would never reveal what his face looked like, even now. I said I didn't know. I told the police that. But I did know.

I never knew what she was thinking, even before she was attacked. Once she was blind, at least I knew what she saw. There were patches of time, days and months, as well as seasons I couldn't remember.

Since then, I have willed myself into selective amnesia, and one day I hope to forget her, what happened to her, just before I forget myself, who I am, who I used to be. Sometimes I am taken off guard by the way the light falls on a woman's hair, the city lights, the actresses' faces in the photos at the old theater where even as a young man I failed miserably. And the actresses ran to me, practically ran into me, thinking I was a genius and could make or break their careers, asking what they should do—not just on stage—but with their lives, long after the play was over. "Can my sister have your eyes?" I wanted to say because they had shut their eyes to everything except themselves, and therefore no longer needed to see. Even before my sister was blinded, she seemed to perceive everyone but her.

"The man in the mask?" she used to ask me. "Why did he do it? Why do you think he chose me? What could he have been thinking when he did that?"

When I first saw the x-rays of my actress's broken hand, in my mind, the stage grew dark. Then, when the light returned, it matched the color of the sky outside of the hospital windows—a gray blue so pale it was almost white. Upon waking, just before she realized we were not in the theater anymore, her stifled cries were as real as the new plaster cast resting in its sling. After she refused to file a police report, the nurses helped her down from the bed and into the wheelchair to escort her out of the hospital. Shortly after, I helped her up the flight of steps leading to the rooms above the theater stage where old set designs were pinned against crumbling walls.

That night while she slept I moved the props across the theater floor, attempting to erase the boundaries of the old stage. After creating a lighting machine to cast a blue flame, using a red light and orange cloth, I tacked a faded silk sky high above the lights where the ceiling once was. I wanted to make the sun rise and set above my audience, who would now be a part of the stage. Sometimes I asked actors and members of the chorus to sing amongst the audience, and the chorus would suddenly burst into song among startled people. Mechanical gulls suspended on fine wire soared beneath the silk sky just before real doves were released into the theater. I changed the light to violet, casting strange angular shadows on upturned noses, spotlights suddenly focusing upon certain faces in the crowd, the colored light making painted lips seem black or gray.

In my mind, I saw it all—every scene I was creating— the play I had produced so long ago.

In the fan's wake, beneath the massive blades, the splendid white banners rippled like waves across the ocean. Parallel to the footlights, my actress bowed as the teal backdrops fell away, revealing a garden in front of a distant painted ocean, fake roses of yellow and red and blue fading on their trellis. The painted ocean background was wheeled away to reveal a hidden stage within the stage so that behind the garden was a pastel washroom beside a red kitchen where prison bars cast shadows across my actress's luminous face.

Lights blazed harshly. Shadows streamed the stage, the light flattening the large painted gray men in the garden, the human statues who now opened their eyes, blinking at the audience in wide-eyed wonder. In the reflection of the large mirror, candles cluttered tables heavy with giant irises in silver or lead-crystal vases. I wanted to dazzle the audience. It was one of the few things I knew how to do—to put on a huge spectacle of romance—to take them up high before I tore them down with the opposite of romance. The crystal vases fractured the spotlight, making dazzling prisms reflected in the mirror that faced my actress as she undressed for bed as if no one was watching her gown falling, her bra coming undone, the delicate straps tangling slightly around the agile fingers of her unbroken hand.

Even the women grew silent. The men forgot to breathe.

Silence—this silence I created—disarmed the audience in the rose light that faded from blue to black before my actress, who still played the part of my sister, stumbled across the room just before all the lights went out—on stage and off. A woman screamed, and then the silence returned, haunting the darkness. The male statues in the garden kissed like lovers before my actress and my sister traded identities that night.

However, my sister did not yet know that play was about her—not until weeks later when the nurses turned on the radio at the hospital and she heard details of the nonexistent plot rehashed in a scathing review.

"You robbed me of me," she later said, weeks before she took her own life. "You took me from me," she whispered, as if I were the one who blinded her, not the masked man who was so quick and so skillful with his knife.

Would it kill me to kill her on stage, night after night?

Part of my conscience was already gone, beyond any metaphoric death. Besides, although I did not believe in art as therapy when traditional narratives and dialogues and happy endings were involved, I knew it could only heal me and make me feel more alive to find ways to face the truth of irrational violence. The illogical nature of animalistic destruction was the demon inside all man, the demon that had invaded my childhood home.

ACKNOWLEDGMENTS

Grateful acknowledgment is made to the editors, readers, and supporters of the following publications in which some of these stories have appeared, sometimes in slightly different versions:

Denver Quarterly: "The Glass Girl," reprinted in *PP/FF: An Anthology*;
Fugue: "Chains";
Lake Effect: "Paints and Papers";
The Literary Review: "Locked Doors";
Mississippi Review: "Dummy";
North American Review: "Warnings";
The Seattle Review: "Shrike";
Tarpaulin Sky: "Allison's Idea";
The Tusculum Review: "Vision of Mirrors";
Vox: "Murder on the Pasture";
Yalobusha Review: "Call Me Linda".

Also, thanks to the Christopher Isherwood Foundation for granting me a fellowship and to the University of North Carolina at Charlotte. Thanks to Peter Conners and everyone at BOA for their kindness, hard work, and impressive knowledge of the literary arts. Thanks to Ted Pelton of Starcherone Books for encouragement. Finally, thanks to friends and family for being there for me over the years—a special "shout out" to Mom, Dad, Lori, Megan, and Daniel, as well as Anna Shapiro and the Shapiro family.

About the Author

The oldest of four children, Aimee Parkison was born in Durant, Oklahoma. She currently resides in Charlotte, North Carolina. Parkison has received a Christopher Isherwood Fellowship, a Writers at Work Fellowship, and a Kurt Vonnegut Fiction Prize. When she's not reading, writing, playing surrealist word games, daydreaming, journaling, or teaching, she's usually hanging out at local coffee shops with her husband Abelardo, playing video games, spending time with her four cats, or enjoying a glass of red wine.

Parkison writes fiction and poetry. She has an MFA from Cornell University and is an Associate Professor of English at The University of North Carolina at Charlotte, where she teaches creative writing. Just after she finished graduate school, her first story collection, *Woman with Dark Horses*, won the first annual Starcherone Fiction Prize. Parkison's work has been nominated for a Pushcart Prize and has appeared in numerous magazines, including *Feminist Studies*, *Mississippi Review*, *North American Review*, *Cimarron Review*, *Quarterly West*, *Santa Monica Review*, *Other Voices*, *Lake Effect*, *Tarpaulin Sky*, *PMS*, *5AM*, *Sow's Ear Poetry Review*, *Hayden's Ferry Review*, *So to Speak*, *Nimrod*, *The Literary Review*, *Crab Orchard Review*, *Fiction International*, *Seattle Review*, and *Denver Quarterly*.

BOA Editions, Ltd.
American Reader Series

No. 1 *Christmas at the Four Corners of the Earth*
Prose by Blaise Cendrars
Translated by Bertrand Mathieu

No. 2 *Pig Notes & Dumb Music: Prose on Poetry*
By William Heyen

No. 3 *After-Images: Autobiographical Sketches*
By W. D. Snodgrass

No. 4 *Walking Light: Memoirs and Essays on Poetry*
By Stephen Dunn

No. 5 *To Sound Like Yourself: Essays on Poetry*
By W. D. Snodgrass

No. 6 *You Alone Are Real to Me: Remembering Rainer Maria Rilke*
By Lou Andreas-Salomé

No. 7 *Breaking the Alabaster Jar: Conversations with Li-Young Lee*
Edited by Earl G. Ingersoll

No. 8 *I Carry A Hammer In My Pocket For Occasions Such As These*
By Anthony Tognazzini

No. 9 *Unlucky Lucky Days*
By Daniel Grandbois

No. 10 *Glass Grapes and Other Stories*
By Martha Ronk

No. 11 *Meat Eaters & Plant Eaters*
       By Jessica Treat

No. 12 *On the Winding Stair*
       By Joanna Howard

No. 13 *Cradle Book*
       By Craig Morgan Teicher

No. 14 *In the Time of the Girls*
       By Anne Germanacos

No. 15 *This New and Poisonous Air*
       By Adam McOmber

No. 16 *To Assume a Pleasing Shape*
       By Joseph Salvatore

No. 17 *The Innocent Party*
       By Aimee Parkison

Colophon

The Innocent Party, stories by Aimee Parkison, is set in Monotype Dante. First created in metal type in the mid-1950s and digitalized in the 1990s, it is the result of a collaboration between Giovanni Mardersteig—a printer, book designer, and typeface artist renowned for the work he produced at Officina Bodoni and Stamperia Valdònega in Italy—and Charles Malin, one of the great punch-cutters of the twentieth century.

The publication of this book is made possible, in part, by the special support of the following individuals:

Anonymous

June C. Baker

Anne Germanacos

Suzanne Gouvernet

Robin, Hollon & Casey Hursh, *in memory of Peter Hursh*

X .J. & Dorothy M. Kennedy

Katherine Lederer

Boo Poulin

Deborah Ronnen & Sherm Levey

Steven O. Russell & Phyllis Rifkin Russell

Glenn & Helen William

Printed in the USA
CPSIA information can be obtained
at www.ICGtesting.com
JSHW022344140824
68134JS00019B/1669